For more than forty years,
Yearling has been the leading name
in classic and award-winning literature
for young readers.

Yearling books feature children's
favorite authors and characters,
providing dynamic stories of adventure,
humor, history, mystery, and fantasy.

Trust Yearling paperbacks to entertain,
inspire, and promote the love of reading
in all children.

OTHER YEARLING BOOKS
YOU WILL ENJOY

BOSTON JANE: AN ADVENTURE, *Jennifer L. Holm*

PENNY FROM HEAVEN, *Jennifer L. Holm*

HATTIE BIG SKY, *Kirby Larson*

LIZZIE BRIGHT AND THE BUCKMINSTER BOY
Gary D. Schmidt

THE MISADVENTURES OF MAUDE MARCH
Audrey Couloumbis

BELLE PRATER'S BOY, *Ruth White*

Boston Jane

WILDERNESS DAYS

JENNIFER L. HOLM

A YEARLING BOOK

Copyright © 2002 by Jennifer L. Holm

All rights reserved. Published in the United States by Yearling, an imprint of Random House Children's Books, a division of Random House, Inc., New York. Originally published in hardcover in the United States by HarperCollins Children's Books, a division of HarperCollins Publishers, New York, in 2002.

Yearling and the jumping horse design are registered trademarks of Random House, Inc.

Visit us on the Web! www.randomhouse.com/kids

Educators and librarians, for a variety of teaching tools, visit us at www.randomhouse.com/teachers

Library of Congress Cataloging-in-Publication Data
Holm, Jennifer L.
Boston Jane : wilderness days / by Jennifer L. Holm. — 1st trade pbk. ed.
p. cm.
Sequel to: Boston Jane: an adventure.
Sequel: Boston Jane: the claim.
Summary: Far from her native Philadelphia, Miss Jane Peck continues to prove that she is more than an etiquette-schooled graduate of Miss Hepplewhite's Young Ladies Academy as she braves the untamed wilderness of Washington Territory in the mid 1850s.
ISBN 978-0-375-86205-2 (trade pbk.) — ISBN 978-0-375-96205-9 (lib. bdg.) — ISBN 978-0-375-89400-8 (e-book)
[1. Frontier and pioneer life—Washington (State)—Fiction. 2. Washington Territory—History—19th century—Fiction. 3. Etiquette—Fiction. 4. Orphans—Fiction. 5. Chinook Indians—Fiction. 6. Indians of North America—Washington (State)—Fiction.] I. Title.
PZ7.H732226Bs 2010
[Fic]—dc22
2009005107

Printed in the United States of America

First Yearling Edition

Random House Children's Books supports the First Amendment and celebrates the right to read.

ACKNOWLEDGMENTS

A lot of very kind people helped Jane find her way in the wilderness.

I would like to thank Gary Johnson, chairman of the Chinook Tribe, for his continued support and advice. His suggestions have made this a better book and me a better writer. Likewise, I'd like to thank David Youckton, chairman of the Chehalis Tribe, for his invaluable counsel, as well as Trudy Marcellay and Hazel Pete for their generous assistance with Chehalis history. Also, James A. Hanson, Ph.D., historian at the Museum of the Fur Trade, helped me add flavor and twang to Mr. Russell's story.

A big shout out to the usual suspects—my brother Matt; my husband, Jonathan; my agent, Jill Grinberg; my folks; Paul and Ginny Merz; my uncle Tommy Hearn—the most encouraging librarian ever; the fabulous Kristin Marang; and especially the fellow authors who've kept me going—particularly Brian Selznick, Shana Corey, and Audrey Couloumbis.

For my brother Matt—
If he were lost in the wilderness,
he'd probably just build a tree fort.

There is great danger of the young and ardent doing injustice to their companions by magnifying trifles, drawing large conclusions from small premises, and judging from a partial knowledge of facts.

—THE YOUNG LADY'S FRIEND (1836),
By a Lady

Boston Jane

WILDERNESS DAYS

CHAPTER ONE

or,
The Luckiest Girl

It was a sweet September day on the beach, much like the day I'd first sailed into Shoalwater Bay that April. The sun was skipping across the water, and the sky was a bright arc of blue racing to impossibly tall green trees. And for the first time since arriving on this wild stretch of wilderness, I felt lucky again.

You see, I had survived these many months in the company of rough men and Chinook Indians, not to mention a flea-ridden hound, and while it was true that my wardrobe had suffered greatly, one might say that my person had thrived. I had made friends. I had started an oyster business. I had survived endless calamity: six months of seasickness on the voyage from Philadelphia, a near-drowning, a fall from a cliff, and a smallpox outbreak. What was there to stop me now?

Although a life on the rugged frontier of the Washington Territory was not recommended for a proper young lady of sixteen, especially in the absence of a suitable chaperone, I intended to try it.

After all, I did make the best pies on Shoalwater Bay. And striding up the beach toward me was a man who appreciated them.

"Jane!"

He had the bluest eyes I had ever seen, bluer than the water of the bay behind him. A schooner, the *Hetty*, was anchored not far out, and it was the reason I had packed all my belongings and was standing beside my trunk. The same schooner had brought Jehu Scudder back to the bay after a prolonged absence. Indeed, when Jehu left, I had doubted that I would ever see him again.

"Jane," Jehu said gruffly, his thick black hair brushing his shoulders, his eyes glowing in his tanned face. I had last seen him nearly two months ago, at which time I had hurt his feelings, and sailor that he was, he had vowed to sail as far away as China to be rid of me.

"Jehu," I replied, nervously pushing a sticky tangle of red curls off my cheeks.

He shook his head. "You're looking well, Miss Peck."

"As are you, Mr. Scudder," I replied, my voice light.

We stood there for a moment just looking at each other, the soft bay air brushing between us like a ribbon. Without thinking, I took a step forward, toward him, until I was so close that I breathed the scent of the saltwater on his skin. And all at once I remembered that night, those stars, his cheek close to mine.

"Boston Jane! Boston Jane!" a small voice behind me cried.

Sootie, a Chinook girl who had become dear to me, came rushing down the beach, little legs pumping, her feet wet from the tide pool in which she had been playing. She was waving a particularly large clamshell at me, of the sort the Chinook children often fashioned into dolls.

"Look what I found!" she said, eyeing Jehu.

"Sootie," I said, smoothing back her thick black hair. "You remember Captain Scudder? He was the first mate on the *Lady Luck*, the ship that brought me here from Philadelphia."

Sootie clutched the skirts of my blue calico dress and hid behind them shyly, peeking out at Jehu with her bright brown eyes. Her mother, my friend Suis, had died in the summer smallpox outbreak, and since then Sootie had spent a great deal of time in my company.

Jehu crouched down next to her, admiring her find. "That's a real nice shell you have there."

She grinned flirtatiously at him, exposing a gap where one of her new front teeth was coming in.

Jehu grinned right back and squinted up at me from where he knelt. "I see you took my advice about wearing blue. Although I did like that Chinook skirt of yours," he teased, his Boston accent dry as a burr.

The cedar bark skirt in question, while very comfortable, had left my legs quite bare. "That skirt was hardly proper, Jehu," I rebuked him gently.

At this, his lips tightened and a shuttered look came across his face. The thick angry scar on his cheek twitched in a familiar way. He hunched his shoulders forward and stood up, deliberately looking somewhere over my shoulder. "Ah, yes, proper."

I bit my lip and stepped back. I had little doubt as to what was causing this sudden transformation. I had rejected his affections, as I had been engaged to another man.

"So tell me, how is your new husband?" he asked in a clipped voice.

"Jehu," I said quickly.

He turned from me and stared angrily out at the smooth bay. "If you'll excuse me, I've got supplies to deliver," he said tersely, and then he turned on his booted heel and strode quickly down the beach away from me.

I took a step forward, Sootie's arms tight around my legs. What was I to do? Miss Hepplewhite, my instructor at the Young Ladies Academy in Philadelphia, had a great number of opinions on the proper behavior of a young lady. I had discovered, however, that many of her careful instructions were sorely lacking when it came to surviving on the frontier. There was not much call for pouring tea or embroidering handkerchiefs in the wilds of Shoalwater Bay. And I certainly didn't recall any helpful hints on how to prevent the only man one had ever kissed from storming away for the second time in one's life. So I did something that I was sure would have shocked my old teacher.

I shouted.

"I didn't marry him!"

He froze and then turned back toward me, walking fast. He grabbed my shoulders and looked down into my eyes.

"You didn't?" Something indefinable flickered across his face.

"It seems that Mr. Baldt already had a wife."

Jehu slapped his thigh triumphantly. "I knew he was no good!"

The difficulties of this year, 1854, had culminated in the sad discovery that the man I had sailed around two continents to marry, William Baldt, had married another before I could arrive. Papa would not have been surprised. Like Jehu, he had a very poor opinion of William Baldt.

"Janey," my white-bearded papa had told me firmly when I declared my intention to accept Mr. Baldt's proposal, "you are transfixed with William for the wrong reasons. There's nothing for you out on that frontier. It's dangerous. There are plenty of eligible young bachelors right here in Philadelphia. There's no call to follow one out west, especially one with no sense."

I confess that I couldn't help but wonder what Papa would think of Jehu. My sweet surgeon father had always been fond of sailors. Why, they were generally his best clients, considering the number of cracked heads that required stitching from drunken bar brawls.

"You're leaving then?" Jehu asked quietly, gesturing to my trunk on the beach.

That morning upon waking I'd had every intention of leaving Shoalwater Bay and all of its inhabitants behind me. After my engagement to William Baldt had fallen apart two weeks earlier, I had arranged for passage back to San Francisco on the schooner *Hetty*, which was due to arrive with supplies. I had bidden my farewells and taken my trunk down to the beach that morning fully expecting to depart the shores of the bay forever.

But as I had watched the *Hetty* sail in, and considered all I had been through—and survived—I had realized that I could follow my sweet papa's advice, and make my own luck right here in Shoalwater Bay.

"Are you going away, Boston Jane?" Sootie asked anxiously, clutching me fiercely around the legs, as if by force alone she could prevent my departure.

Speak up, Janey. Say what's on your mind, Papa always said.

I looked into Jehu's clear eyes, and said to Sootie, my voice shaking slightly, "No. I'm not going anywhere."

Papa, I thought, would be so proud of me.

Jehu's shoulders seemed to relax. Was that a hint of admiration in his eyes?

Sootie smiled up at me. "Oh good! Now I can show you how to make me a dolly." She tugged at my hand.

Jehu snapped his fingers. "I almost forgot. I've got something for you," he said, fishing in the leather satchel slung over his shoulder and pulling out a letter. The handwriting was familiar.

"It's a letter—" he began.

"From Papa!" I cried, snatching it from his fingers.

"Picked it up from a passing ship. Got a few letters for Swan, and one for Russell, too."

The mail was a random enterprise, with letters generally delivered by passing ships. I had not received a letter from Papa since arriving on Shoalwater Bay. Then again, I had not written Papa for several months now, and as I turned the letter over in my hand, I felt a rush of guilt.

Although he had not prevented my trip, Papa had made it

clear that he did not think highly of William Baldt, and I had delayed writing him from shame when William had not met me upon my arrival. I had intended to write him after William showed up and we were married. Then the engagement had been broken, and as I had thought to return home, there was no need for a letter. Now perhaps I would write and persuade Papa to join me. The settlement could most certainly use a proper physician.

Papa. How I missed his booming laugh. His warm eyes. His ability to finish off one of Mrs. Parker's cherry pies in a single sitting.

I recalled the way his mustache turned up at the corners when he smiled, and how he never turned away patients, not even when they stumbled onto our doorstep in the middle of the night.

And most of all, I recalled how when I was a little girl he would stand at the bottom of the stairs and call: "Where is my favorite daughter?"

It was our little ritual. I would throw back the covers on my four-poster bed, rush down the hall in my bare feet, and peer down at him from the top of the stairs.

"She is right here!" I would say. "And she is your *only* daughter!"

He would shake his head at me, his eyes crinkling with amusement, and more often than not, he would roar with laughter at the picture I presented.

"You're not my Janey! My Janey never sleeps through breakfast! My Janey's hair is never tangled."

It had always just been Papa and me. And, of course, Mrs.

Parker, our kindly housekeeper, who had wiped away every childhood tear with her worn apron. They were all the family I had ever known.

I took the letter and carefully, slowly unfolded it, intending to savor every word.

February 15, 1854

My sweet Janey,

> *You cannot know how it pains me to write this letter. How I would wish, rather, for one last chance to tell you that you are my favorite daughter.*

> *I have been suffering from consumption these past months. Although it broke my heart to let you go, I knew that you would be safer away. I'm quite afraid that I could not bear the thought of you succumbing to this wretched illness as well. As such, I have left instructions for my solicitor, Mr. Edmonds, to send you this letter upon my death.*

> *It has been a great comfort to me to know that you have begun a new life with William, and I wish you every happiness, my dearest girl. It was selfish of me to stand in your way those last months you were at home. Please forgive an old man who could not bear to watch his little girl grow up and leave his house to start a home of her own. Your happiness is all I have ever longed for since you came into my life as a red-haired,*

smiling infant with a penchant for sucking on my thumb. Your bright face was the only thing that made life possible for me after your mother's death.

In regard to my estate, I have directed that Mr. Edmonds sell the house on Walnut Street and give a portion of the funds to Mrs. Parker, who may continue on as housekeeper for the new owner if she so wishes. The rest of the money shall be deposited in your account at the bank in San Francisco. I fear that I have not left you a fortune, my dear, but perhaps it will be enough to buy you some small thing that your heart desires.

I have always loved you, Janey—both the little girl who ran around with a pie-stained apron and tangled hair, and the elegant young lady you have become.

Take greatest care of yourself, my dearest daughter. Listen to your heart, and you will find your way.

Remember—you make your own luck.

Love, Papa

When I looked up, Jehu was standing there, watching me carefully.

"Bad news?"

I shook my head wordlessly. Above us a gull squawked hoarsely, and as if it were yesterday I recalled the way Papa's coughing had filled the house at night, and how he had at first forbidden me to travel west to marry William. What horrible fights we had had! And then I recalled how, the morning after a visit by a fellow physician, Papa's resistance had abruptly evaporated, and he had given me his permission to marry.

He had known he was dying! That was why he had let me go.

I felt a pain deep in my stomach, sharp as the hurtful words I had spoken to my sweet papa, and staggered forward.

"Boston Jane?" Sootie asked nervously, looking between Jehu and me.

Jehu's eyes widened in alarm. "Jane, what is it?" he asked urgently, grabbing my shoulders.

"Papa's dead."

"Oh, Jane." Jehu's voice echoed in my head.

And then I did precisely what Miss Hepplewhite would have recommended in just such a situation.

I fainted.

CHAPTER TWO

or,

All Alone in the World

When I came to, I found myself on a hard bunk in a filthy, flea-ridden cabin.

The settlement at Shoalwater Bay was barely a settlement at all. In the center of a muddy clearing, up from the winding beach, stood Mr. Russell's pioneer cabin, which doubled as a trading post—and inside it I now lay. A slender stream running alongside the cabin led to the Chinook village, where my friends Keer-ukso and Chief Toke and Sootie lived. Near a spot on the stream where the Chinooks liked to gather water was a small rustic chapel. There Father Joseph, a French Catholic missionary, preached and lived. Farther up the bay, a pioneer named M'Carty and his Chinook wife had a cabin.

Mr. Russell's cabin had been my home, albeit a poor excuse for one, since arriving on the bay in April. I had been obliged to take up residence there because my former betrothed had abandoned me, without bothering to arrange suitable accommodations. The inside of the cabin consisted of a ramshackle grouping of wooden bunks lining two walls, a rickety set of shelves that contained trading supplies, and a sawbuck table where meals were generally taken. The floor was hard-packed dirt, and the cabin had a tendency to attract local vermin despite my hard work trying to keep it clean. Then again, the vermin were quite probably attracted by the filthy pioneer men, who thought it perfectly reasonable to take a bath once a month. Any pioneer man passing through Shoalwater Bay looking to make his fortune was welcome to stay in the cabin where I resided. Needless to say, I was now rather unfortunately used to the sound of snoring men.

"Jane," a deep voice said, and I looked up to see the worried, bearded face of Mr. Swan, a decidedly curious man who had come to the bay all the way from Boston to study the Chinook Indians. His spectacles were balanced precariously on his bulbous nose as he surveyed me anxiously. He had a thick white beard and flyaway hair. This eccentric, excitable older man had been almost like a father to me in the time that I'd resided here on Shoalwater Bay.

A father.

I remembered at once the reason I was lying here and squeezed my eyes shut. Papa was dead. My own sweet papa. Hot tears slipped from my eyes, and I felt gasps rising in my throat.

"Oh, my dear girl," Mr. Swan said awkwardly, smoothing back my untidy red hair. "I am so terribly sorry."

But something inside of me was draining out, falling away, and although I heard the concern in his voice, my mouth couldn't form any words. All I could think was that Papa was gone. It was too much. Too much to live, knowing that I was all alone in this cold, lonely world.

I turned away and closed my eyes.

When I next was aware of opening my eyes, the wind hissed softly through the tiny window, promising cold days ahead. It was September, but it looked the same as when I had first arrived in April. Nothing but gray gloom in all directions and endless rain in this soggy place in the middle of nowhere.

The rain beat a steady drum on the roof, lulling me, like the clip-clop sound of carriages going up and down the cobble-stones of Walnut Street in Philadelphia. The men moved about the cabin, their voices hushed murmurs. I heard a crackle and hiss, smelled the scent of salt pork frying. I had been in bed for three days now, or was it four? How easily time slipped away. Sometimes it felt like I had been forever in this wet, musty place. It was better—yes, better—to simply close my eyes and ignore all the voices calling me steadily, intruding on this quiet, urging me to get up, to go on, to live. Better to ignore Jehu's warm hand holding mine, his fingers smoothing down my hair, tangling in my curls like a brush.

If I closed my eyes, it all came rushing back. If I strained hard with my heart, I could hear the life I had left behind so long ago. It was so easy, really, to simply slip away, slip back to Walnut Street. One moment I was on the hard bunk in Mr. Russell's cabin and the next I was on my childhood bed, the four posts rising around me like comforting sentries, the mattress soft as a cloud. Everything so very warm and dry and dear.

A familiar voice called up to my window.

Come on, Jane!

Was that my childhood playmate Jebediah Parker calling me to come out and play? To run up and down Walnut Street and toss apples and chase carriages and throw pats of manure?

And that smell, so like the warm scents that used to drift up from Mrs. Parker's kitchen. Was she making roast pork and apples for supper? Yes, I must be in the kitchen, next to the stove, the smells so strong and sweet that my mouth watered. And what was that other smell? That woodsy smell drifting on the air? I squeezed my eyes, memory straining now, and recognized Papa's tobacco!

"Janey," Papa said, leaning over me, his eyes full of laughter. "It's time for supper."

I opened my mouth to tell him how much I missed him, how very much, and then Mr. Swan's face swam into view, a pipe balanced in his mouth, the smoke rising in curls. He was holding a steaming bowl.

"Supper. I've made my famous fisherman's pudding." He swallowed hard, worry etching lines in his face. "Please, my dear, you must eat something," he pleaded in a strained voice.

But how could I eat when Papa would never take another bite again? When he would never stroll down the street, or puff on his pipe, or roar with laughter, because he was buried in the cold, cold ground. A heavy, leaden feeling pushed down on my chest, and I closed my eyes and felt myself drift away, tugged like a log on the tide, the waves dragging me farther and farther until Mr. Swan's face was a speck on the horizon.

And then he was gone.

All the men of the settlement worried about me.

But there was nothing I could do, you see, except lie there and remember the pallor of Papa's face when I left Philadelphia—how during my final months at home he had coughed and coughed, a cough that racked his chest and left him gasping for air. I couldn't forget how unkind I had been to him, how we had fought so fiercely over my engagement to William Baldt, how I, his only daughter, had abandoned him to follow a useless man west. I had chosen my own selfish desires and left my dear, sweet papa to die alone in Philadelphia.

The men took turns trying to entice me back to the world of the living.

Jehu recited tales of sea voyages taken before he had ever met me, how he had traveled across the seas to China, and how he had seen women in the Sandwich Islands who wore grass skirts. Mr. Swan read from his diary, describing the medicinal properties of plants and the pattern of the tides on Shoalwater Bay. Chief Toke, Sootie's father and the kindly chief of the local Chinooks, brought Sootie, who bounced on the side of the bunk, discussing her doll collection earnestly. And Father Joseph sat by my side, head bowed, whispering soft prayers in French, the words low and comforting like a nursery rhyme. Even Brandywine, Mr. Swan's plump, flea-bitten hound, took time off from begging for food around the campsite to sleep curled up at the foot of the bunk, his cold, wet nose pressed against my feet.

But it was my dear friend Keer-ukso who almost lured me back. His musical voice snaked into my dreams and tugged at me. Maybe it was the sorrow, the deep, aching emptiness that he carried around with him that I recognized, so like my own. He alone, who had recently lost loved ones in the summer outbreak, seemed to understand how difficult it was to hear the sound of life continuing, moving forward so effortlessly, as if Papa had never lived at all. As if the world could go on without his booming laugh or kind eyes.

Keer-ukso sat quietly beside me, chanting softly in Chinook.

"Halo moosum," he whispered, and it sounded like the wind whipping through the cedar trees, the sound washing over me like the fog on the bay.

But then his voice drifted away and I couldn't hear him; it was as if I were too far away.

And maybe I was.

"Dang gal, ya stink worse than a beaver rotting in the sun," a voice said loudly, and I heard the distinct sound of spitting, followed by the soft wet noise of tobacco hitting the floor.

I blinked my eyes open to see Mr. Russell towering over me. When I had first arrived on the bay, this filthy, buckskin-clad, ill-mannered mountain man, much given to spitting tobacco in my general direction, had spent his days ordering me about the cabin as if I were a maid. But as time passed, I had grudgingly come to respect, and, I suppose, admire the gruff, long-whiskered man who ate whatever I placed before him.

"What's going on here, gal? I go away hunting for a few days and come back and find ya lying in bed like a lump when there's mending to be done?" Mr. Russell barked impatiently. "And all these here men have been mollycoddling ya while ya stink up the place!"

I flipped over and stared out the window, watching the rain drop in a steady patter, his voice lost in the swirl of the wind.

"You hear me, gal? I said ya stink!"

Suddenly my blanket was whipped away and the world tilted. Mr. Russell threw me over his shoulder unceremoniously and carried me, dirty blanket in hand, out of the cabin. He dropped me on the rickety front porch in the pouring rain with a resounding thump.

And then he closed the door with a bang and locked it. I lay there in my soggy blanket, stunned.

For the first time in all those long days, I felt a faint glimmer of something rush through me. A hot feeling. Hot and furious.

Anger.

The loathsome man had locked me out of the cabin in the middle of a rainstorm!

I started to pound on the door of the cabin. "Let me in!" I shouted, my voice hoarse from disuse.

I heard him guffawing on the other side of the door. "Gal, ya been rottin' in that bed for nearly two weeks and ya smell worse than Brandywine. Ya ain't coming back in here until yar scrubbed up!"

Even in my dark mood I hardly thought that he should be one to complain of such things. Mr. Russell was notorious for his lack of bathing.

"You horrible man!" I pounded on the door, but all I heard was laughing.

"I see you're finally up."

I whirled around to see Jehu standing there, shaking his head, amusement in his eyes. I clutched my dirty blanket to me and glared.

"That, that—blasted man threw me out of the cabin!" I sputtered furiously.

Jehu squinted at me through the rain dripping from his wet hair. "Seems he did."

Just then Mr. Swan and Keer-ukso appeared.

"Capital! You're up, dear girl," Mr. Swan said in a relieved voice. "We were on the verge of taking Toke's advice and tossing you into the spring." His smile slipped a little as he took in my ratty, tangled hair and my filthy woolen nightdress. "But really, my dear, perhaps you ought to consider a bath."

Jehu raised his eyebrows slightly.

"Oh!" I huffed, and stormed away through the mud.

CHAPTER THREE
or,
The Most Disagreeable Man
in the Territory

The next morning found me sitting on the rickety cabin porch attempting to compose a letter to Papa's solicitor. It had continued to rain during the night, and everything was damp. The ground had turned to mud, and the sky was as gray as a chimney sweep's hat. Another perfectly dreadful day on Shoalwater Bay.

The men's snoring had kept me up most of the night, and every shrieking animal sound startled me. Even Brandywine's light waffling dog snores made me twitch and turn in discomfort. I had lain for hours staring at the ceiling of the cabin on my hard bunk, unease running through my blood like ice. I felt myself adrift in the world. Already motherless, I now had no father, no house to call home, and no kindly Mrs. Parker to dry my tears on her apron. I had nothing at all.

A chunk of black, chewed tobacco landed at my feet with a wet slap.

"Now that yar up," Mr. Russell announced, one gray whisker twitching, "ya can start mending again." He held aloft a crusty-looking shirt with a torn sleeve.

I had done the mending and some cooking around Mr. Russell's cabin in exchange for my board, although considering the shabby conditions, it was clear that he was getting the better bargain.

"Is that all you care about? That you lost your seamstress?"

He shrugged. "Well, I reckon I missed the cooking, too. Ya don't have much of a hang for it, but I've et worse."

"I'm not your maid!" I shouted.

"That don't shine with me." He pointed at me sharply. "Ya work if ya want a roof over yer head."

He flung the torn shirt at me, but I deliberately stepped back and watched it fall on the muddy ground. "Yar gonna have to wash it now, too, ya stubborn gal. And supper best be on the table tonight," he said. Then he shambled away. "And make one of them pies," he added over his shoulder.

I waited until he was out of sight before grabbing up the shirt and stomping into the cabin to prepare supper.

"I should make him a mud pie," I muttered to myself, sorely tempted to do just that.

As I measured and sifted and stirred, I fumed. Mr. Russell was plainly the most disagreeable man in the entire territory. He was everything I despised in this foul, wet place. He spent every waking moment spitting his filthy tobacco. He guzzled whiskey and spoke in grunts. Not to mention, I was convinced he was the principal reason there were so many fleas in the cabin.

He wouldn't know a good manner if it ran up the leg of his disgusting buckskin trousers and bit him. And to think that I had once considered him a good-hearted man! I had been fooled by his small kindnesses to me, such as the time the bar of lavender soap mysteriously appeared among my belongings shortly after Mr. Russell had returned from Astoria. But I saw the truth now: he was just a mean, selfish, ignorant man who cared for no one but himself. After all, what kind of man throws a young lady into the rain in little more than a woolen nightgown? What kind of a man—

"Are you trying to kill that dough?" a voice asked mildly. "I'll shoot it if you want me to put it out of its misery."

It was Jehu. He took two long-legged strides over to the table and eyed my handiwork. I had been so consumed by my anger toward Mr. Russell that the piecrust I had been fashioning had been rolled flat as a pocket-handkerchief.

"Blasted Mr. Russell," I muttered, gathering up the beaten dough and patting it back into a ball.

Jehu dragged up a chair and watched me.

"Do you know that I have a bruise from where he dropped me on the porch?" I exploded.

Jehu's mouth turned up in a small grin. "Really? Where?"

"You're just as bad as him! There is not a single decent gentleman in the whole of this wretched territory!" I seethed, flattening the dough again with the rolling pin, as if the act alone

21

would smooth out all the wrinkles in my life. "I hate this place. I don't even know why I'm here. I'll never be dry again, not to mention I'll never get a moment's sleep from all the snoring, and—"

"I haven't seen my father since he laid open my cheek with that horse harness," Jehu said quietly.

My hands went still.

He rubbed the thick, angry scar on his cheek. "That was, well, nearly ten years ago now. Don't really know for sure if he's even alive."

His eyes met mine across the emptiness of the cabin, and I felt myself bite back tears.

Oh, Papa.

Just then the door banged open. It was Keer-ukso.

"This is not a barn!" I shouted, my grief turning to fury in a rush.

The two men exchanged a look, and Keer-ukso closed the door carefully, then sat down on a bench near Jehu. Keer-ukso meant crooked nose in Chinook. As was the Chinook custom, he had changed his name after some of his family had died in the summer outbreak. The Chinook believe that the ghosts of the dead can't haunt you if you change your name. Still, in my mind he would always be the name I first knew him by and which suited him so well, Handsome Jim.

For, you see, he was truly the most handsome young man I had ever been acquainted with in my entire life. He had long, thick black hair, lovely eyes, and a muscled body. He was also a kind, sweet friend who always managed to make me laugh. Well, usually he did. For I found nothing amusing about him reaching into the bowl of berries I had set aside for the pie. I slapped his hand away.

Jehu rolled his eyes.

"Mr. Russell say you cook pie, Boston Jane," Keer-ukso said, looking affronted.

"Oh, did he?" I asked in a tight voice.

"Jane's a little frustrated with Mr. Russell right now," Jehu explained helpfully.

"Frustrated!" I huffed. "Frustrated is living in a cabin where fleas are permanent residents! Frustrated is being surrounded by filthy, snoring strangers! Frustrated is being stuck in this infernal wilderness where it never stops raining. Believe me, I am frustrated by a great many things, but Mr. Russell is not one of them."

"So if you're not frustrated, what are you?" Jehu asked, reaching for a berry.

I grabbed the overworked, gray lump of dough and flung it in the men's general direction. It struck Jehu's chest with a thump before landing on Keer-ukso.

"Is this pie?" Keer-ukso asked, an astonished look on his face.

"Yes! It's the blasted pie," I shouted, and stomped to the door of the cabin. "And for your information, Mr. Scudder, I'm not frustrated with Mr. Russell." I paused for effect. "I'm furious!"

And with that I slammed the cabin door, and practically ran down the path alongside the slender stream that led to the

Chinook village, my blood racing. I passed by Father Joseph's small chapel and saw him raise a hand in greeting, but I didn't stop. I kept walking fast, my heart pounding, and it wasn't until I saw the large wooden buildings rising from the trees that I felt my heart slow down to a reasonable thump.

Chief Toke's village consisted of several large cedar lodges. The lodges were quite comfortable dwellings, and much more spacious, not to mention cleaner, than the pioneer cabins. As I entered the village, I saw the Chinooks going about their daily routines. They were a copper-skinned people, with thick black hair. Some of them, like Sootie, had slanted foreheads from having been placed in a cradleboard as a baby. A slanted forehead was a mark of distinction.

The men wore the same style of clothes as the pioneers, although some of the older men wore blankets. In addition to wearing calico dresses, the women sometimes wore skirts constructed of strips of twisted cedar bark.

Some of the Chinooks shouted my name in greeting.

"Boston Jane!"

Although I was from Philadelphia, the Chinooks referred to the Americans as *Boston tillicums* or *Boston people*, as the first American ships to arrive on the bay were from Boston.

I discovered Sootie finally behind one of the lodges with two boys, ensconced in a game. The little girl had often turned to me for comfort in the weeks following her mother's death, but now I found that our roles were reversed. From the grin on Sootie's face, it was clear to see she was holding her own with the two lads, who, I should say, looked particularly annoyed.

One of the boys stood up and walked away in disgust. He was followed a moment later by the other boy, who had a rather dejected expression on his face.

"You won, Sootie?" I asked.

A bright smile wreathed her face. "Boston Jane!"

"What did you win?" I crouched down next to her, surveying the small pile of treasures.

Sootie held up pretty smooth stones, glass beads, and a glossy black feather. I admired them dutifully and couldn't help but notice that her face had the same satisfied look that her mother's had had when she'd made a good trade. The Chinooks were great traders, and wealth was a sign of status. The *tyee,* or chief, was generally the wealthiest person.

She displayed a piece of purple velvet that she had also won. "Will you make me a new dress for dolly?" Sootie asked, tugging at the blue calico fabric of my dress. "Like your Boston dress?"

I nodded. "I believe I can do that."

Sootie pointed to my collar with a critical eye. "With that, too."

"Very well."

"And this," she added, touching the scallop of lace at my wrist.

I laughed. "You should be a fashion editor for *Godey's Lady's Book.*"

"What is that?" she asked.

"That is a lady who thinks about dresses all day!"

"Oh yes!" she said happily.

I stood up, extending my hand. "Shall we go back to your lodge and get started on this new wardrobe?"

She gathered her treasures into her skirt, then she put her small, trusting hand in mine, and together we walked to her lodge.

The cedar lodge was quite large, and we entered it by slipping through an opening near the ground. Firepits lined the center of the lodge, and cedar planks that could be shifted to allow smoke to escape served as the roof. The Chinooks often laid salmon on a grid of poles beneath the ceiling in order to smoke the fish—a very clever idea in my opinion.

Huge bunklike structures, platforms really, were built along the interior walls, and it was upon these that families lived. Rush mats lined the floors, which proved very handy in keeping the dust down. I had adopted the Chinook method of using mats in the cabin, and though the dust was less of a problem, the men still helpfully tromped in huge bootfuls of caked mud. It was fair to say that Chief Toke's tidy lodge was a vast improvement on Mr. Russell's cabin.

It was nearly suppertime, and there were men gathered around the fire roasting salmon. The sight of men preparing supper for their families still surprised me after all these months, although it was quite usual for the Chinooks.

I was startled to see Mr. Russell conferring with Chief Toke on a platform at the other end of the lodge. The kindly chief very much reminded me of a judge in Philadelphia who had been friends with Papa.

"Thought you were supposed to be fixing supper, gal," Mr. Russell said loudly.

I opened my mouth to say I had no intention of fixing supper for such a disagreeable man when Sootie piped up in a clear voice.

"Boston Jane is making a dress for my dolly."

"Well, hurry it up," Mr. Russell said. "I want supper ready before sundown."

Sootie took a protective step in front of me and marched right up to Mr. Russell, utterly fearless, and waved the piece of velvet in his face. "You make supper," Sootie said with a firm little shake of her head.

Mr. Russell looked taken aback.

I stifled a laugh, and Chief Toke's dark eyes filled with mirth at his brave little daughter, so very like his late wife.

Mr. Russell shook his head in a bewildered way and then looked at me wryly. "Well, you heard her, gal. Go on and make this little girl a dress. I reckon I'll be fixing supper."

Sootie shot me a triumphant smile.

"I reckon you will, Mr. Russell," I said, and smiled right back at my small defender.

CHAPTER FOUR

or,
Mr. Swan's Gamble

Men began arriving on a daily basis from as far away as Maine, having heard word that a man could earn his fortune in oysters on Shoalwater Bay. They came by horse from the East overland, and by schooner up the coast. Many of the men who had not found gold in California were determined to strike it rich at last, or, at the very least, claim their own land.

In short order we had a retired sea captain, a mason, a carpenter, and a gentleman called Red Charley, who liked to take all the hard-earned money of the other men by selling whiskey at exorbitant prices. I longed for another woman to arrive, but it seemed that fortune hunters were not good husband material. In addition to bathing infrequently at best, the men arriving on Shoalwater Bay were of very questionable character. It was widely suspected that more than one of them was fleeing the law or some other trouble from where he came. None of them brought a wife.

Mr. Russell's cramped cabin could no longer accommodate all the visitors, and there was suddenly a buzz of activity as small cabins were erected and tents pitched along the arch of the bay to house the new arrivals. I was thankful not to have strange men staying in the cabin any longer. Well, except Mr. Swan, Mr. Russell, and Brandywine the hound. There was talk of building a proper store, and one enterprising young man even constructed a nine-pin bowling alley in an abandoned Chinook lodge, where men could be found drinking and bowling and playing card games long into the night.

I kept busy cooking and cleaning around the cabin, and for extra money I took in mending and laundry. The laundry was pure drudgery, and after a week of darning socks, sewing holes in sleeves, and cleaning pants that had been on a body for so long they deserved a proper burial, I resolved to pursue something else.

Mr. Swan and I owned an oyster business together. To be clear, he owned a claim on a sizable patch of oysters on the bay, and I owned a sturdy Chinook canoe. Oysters were very popular everywhere in the States, although I found them quite disgusting. Even so, the slimy gray things did bring in a silver dollar apiece in San Francisco, and while harvesting them was hard work, it didn't involve scrubbing bloodstains from collars. We'd had a very successful oyster harvest in July, and I had used some of my earnings to purchase a new pair of boy's boots and blue calico fabric for new dresses. But now my funds were rather low.

I set out looking for Mr. Swan one late October morning.

Men were working hard everywhere, building cabins and mending canoes. As I followed the path that led to Chief Toke's village and then onto the beach where I suspected I'd find Mr. Swan, men called out to me and whistled wolfishly. Jehu saw me coming down the trail, and put down the axe he was using to chop wood.

"I'm looking for Mr. Swan," I said.

He wiped his forehead. His thick black hair was damp with sweat, and it clung to the nape of his neck. "I think he's down on the beach scribbling in his diary."

"What are you doing?" I asked.

"Father Joseph wanted me to build him some more benches. Seems he's hoping to get a bigger parish with all the new arrivals," he said with a knowing wink.

I laughed. Father Joseph had a very difficult time getting the men to come to church. I suspected that if he offered whiskey instead of communion wine, he'd have a full house every week.

Jehu hefted a piece of wood onto the small pile. His arms were muscled from years of working on ships. I stood there for a moment, just watching. I had, of course, seen Jehu around the settlement, but he most often stayed at Chief Toke's lodge. It seemed that he and Keer-ukso were becoming fast friends. Even so, he was a sailor, and I wondered why he was still here on the bay.

"Jehu, what are you doing here anyway? Hasn't the *Hetty* left? Shouldn't you be sailing back to San Francisco or some exotic, faraway place?"

Jehu regarded me appraisingly. "I thought I'd stick around here for a bit. Maybe even put in a claim on a piece of land."

"Hmmf." I was unimpressed. The last man who had tried to tell me about the merits of homesteading had been a scoundrel and a swine. William Baldt had wanted to marry me in order to gain more land, for a single man in the territory could only claim half the amount of land that a married one could. This was the reason he hadn't bothered to wait for me to arrive but had married another woman—he hadn't wanted to lose all that land.

"What about you?" Jehu asked, studying me carefully.

"I want to start oystering again," I said finally.

Like many men, my former betrothed had been very much against a wife's working outside the home, but Jehu just nodded and squinted into the sun, saying nothing.

I swallowed hard, and started walking.

"Jane," he called. "Let me know if you need help."

I turned back and smiled at him gratefully. "I will," I promised.

The gray clouds parted and the sun peeked out, sending shafts of light dancing across the blue expanse of the bay, and I felt my heart lighten. When it wasn't raining, Shoalwater Bay was like a charming young man courting a lady—all smiling and full of good humor.

Just as Jehu said, Mr. Swan was perched upon a fallen log on the beach, sketching in his diary. Mr. Swan was interested in the flora and fauna of the region, so much so that he had, in fact, abandoned a wife and children in Boston to come to Shoalwater Bay to study them. Mr. Swan was rather peculiar, but I was very fond of him.

"Why, hello, my dear," Mr. Swan said cheerily, setting down his pen.

"What are you working on?" I asked. Mr. Swan kept notes and drew pictures in his diary. He had great plans to publish it one day, and I took pains to display interest in it as he was so proud.

He displayed a sketch of a feathery-looking plant. "Toke told me that this plant is quite therapeutic for all manner of skin ailments." His enthusiasm reminded me of Papa, who could talk for hours about an interesting case. "Apparently one is supposed to put the leaf directly on the skin."

"That's very interesting," I replied.

"And this is a salal plant," he explained, turning the page. "They grow very tasty berries. Chief Toke showed me where a lovely patch grows. Perhaps you could make one of your famous pies using the berries one day, my dear?" he asked hopefully.

"I'm sure I could," I said gently, and then turned the conversation to matters at hand. "Mr. Swan, I would like for us to start harvesting oysters again."

He looked at me blankly for a moment and then clapped his hands. "What a capital idea, my dear girl! I'm nearly broke."

I didn't have to ask where his money had gone. Mr. Swan, like every second man in the territory, was afflicted with a costly fondness for his friend, Old Rye. Whiskey.

"Do you know a schooner we can hire?" It was important that a schooner be on the bay on the day of the harvest; otherwise the oysters would go bad before they ever reached San Francisco. "There seems to be a constant stream of them."

He rubbed his beard thoughtfully. "There should be a number arriving, my dear. I'm afraid we shall have to negotiate. We aren't the only ones who need to ship oysters these days. And of course, we shall also have to consider hiring some help. We could always hire some of the pioneers if we can't get any of Toke's people."

"We should hire Chinooks," I said firmly. "They are more skilled, and far more knowledgeable. After all, Chief Toke was the one who helped you find the oyster bed in the first place." I wanted to add that they smelled better than the pioneer men as well. The Chinooks bathed regularly, a custom I had come to appreciate greatly.

"Very well, then. Let's get started," Mr. Swan agreed.

Mr. Swan and I mapped out how much we could pay for our help and the schooner and still turn a profit. The oyster beds were on the bay, and Mr. Swan's claim was marked by a wooden stick with a carved swan. All the men identified their claims in a similar manner.

In order to reach the beds to harvest the oysters, we would use my beautiful Chinook canoe. The canoe, which I had acquired over the summer when bargaining with Suis, was carved from a single cedar log and was over forty feet long, nearly six feet wide, and decorated stem to stern with snail shells. It was a marvel of construction and perfectly suited our purposes.

"If we hire another canoe, my dear, we could easily double our profit," Mr. Swan said, reviewing the figures in his journal.

"But you have no funds to hire another canoe," I said.

His face fell. "Ah, yes, that is an impediment."

I sighed. It made me very nervous, but after a moment's consideration, I said, "I have some money we could use."

Mr. Swan immediately brightened. "Capital, dear girl! It is a gamble, but I have every confidence that it is not a risky one. And you shall be well rewarded for your fortitude."

We determined that we would need at least ten people, including Mr. Swan and me, to man the two canoes and harvest the oysters. All that was left to do was hire the men, the schooner, and the additional canoe.

I could barely fall asleep for excitement, and I was up bright and early the next morning. Mr. Swan was not to be found, so I set out on my own. M'Carty, from farther up the bay, was the first man I approached. Honest and likable, M'Carty was from Tennessee and very plainspoken. He had bought and shipped our oysters during the summer and had a very good relationship with Chief Toke, as he was Toke's son-in-law.

"Sorry, Miss Peck," M'Carty said, puffing on his pipe. "My schooners are booked up for the next three months."

"But we can't wait that long. It will be winter then!"

I had heard the stories of how whole beds of oysters had been lost to a heavy frost the previous winter.

He tilted his head in agreement and looked up, considering. "You should speak to Red Charley. He's got a boat here already."

I grimaced. In addition to the deplorable fact that he provided whiskey to the men of the bay, Red Charley also had the uncommon ability to live in the same shirt for three weeks at a time before bringing it to me to launder. He was a filthy man.

"You know I'd help you out if I could, Jane," M'Carty said with a shrug.

I squared my shoulders and went in search of Red Charley. He lived in a flimsy cabin not far from Chief Toke's village. I worried that he would trade whiskey with the Chinooks, but Father Joseph assured me that he was keeping a hawk eye on the greedy man.

I found the disreputable fellow in his dank little cabin drinking whiskey.

Red Charley grinned toothily when he saw me, his cheeks ruddy and bright as two tomatoes. "Come for the laundry, gal?" He licked his lips in an unsavory way.

I bit my tongue and forced myself to smile at him. "Actually, I'm here to discuss hiring your schooner."

Charley snorted. "You?"

It was disconcerting to be negotiating with the same man whose shirts I washed. "Yes," I said firmly.

He grunted, settled back in his chair, and took a long drink of whiskey. "Don't do business with womenfolk."

"Actually," I said, "Mr. Swan is my partner, and he would be here himself except that he was called away on a very important errand."

Red Charley looked like he didn't believe me. "Swan, eh?"

"Truly," I said.

"Well, I was waiting on some lumber, but how much are you willing to pay?"

My friend Suis had been an excellent trader and had taught me how to bargain, a useful skill on the frontier. I named a sum that I knew to be far too low.

The red-bearded, filthy man chortled. "I can get me ten times that if'n I wait for my lumber." And then he countered with an offer much too high.

"By the time your lumber is cut and ready to load, your schooner could be gone and back with more whiskey," I added and named a price a little higher than my initial offer.

His eyes narrowed in greed, as if calculating his future riches. "That may be so, but that's still too low. Got to pay my crew, after all."

I countered, and named a price a little higher, and then he countered. This game went on for some time until we met in the middle, which had been my intention all along. I was quite pleased with myself as I had come in below the budget I had discussed with Mr. Swan, but I was careful to mask my true feelings.

"You got a deal, gal," Red Charley said, his grin revealing tobacco-stained teeth. He spat in his hand and held it out. "Let's shake on it."

I looked in horror at his hand.

"Come on, gal," Red Charley said, thrusting his hand out farther.

I gingerly placed my hand in his and he pumped it hard. "It's a deal," I said, gritting my own teeth, and then I turned and strode quickly from the cabin and down to the stream, where I threw my hand in the rushing water.

I enlisted Keer-ukso's help as interpreter. My knowledge of the Chinook Jargon, the local trading language on the bay, was limited. The Jargon was mostly Chinook, with some French and English mixed in. Even though some of the Chinooks spoke English, most of them spoke the Jargon, and it was the only common language among the tribes and settlers in the territory.

Keer-ukso was happy to help, and in the end I negotiated for an additional canoe and for the services of eight men. Keer-ukso instructed them to be standing by in two days' time. We were ready.

I related the good news to Mr. Swan after supper.

He had been occupied for the day settling a dispute before guns were drawn. There was no law on the bay, and as Mr. Swan had some experience in legal matters back in Boston, he was most often called upon in situations like this.

"I'm afraid we had to kick Hairy Bill off of the bay," Mr. Swan said with a heavy sigh. "He was caught redhanded with the stolen goods. Been stealing from nearly everyone, judging from what we found in his tent."

"That's terrible," I said, and served him a slice of left-over pie.

"Capital, dear girl!" He took a bite of pie, closing his eyes in delight. "You make the best pie in the territory, my dear."

I smiled. It was almost like being back on Walnut Street with Papa, the two of us eating Mrs. Parker's cherry pie and discussing the day's events.

"Jane," Mr. Swan said.

"Yes?"

Mr. Swan had an expression on his face, the same expression I had seen on Papa's face many times. An expression of pride.

"You did a very fine job negotiating," he said, his eyes meeting mine.

My eyes stung as a I felt a bittersweet rush of emotions—pleasure at being praised by Mr. Swan, and sadness because he reminded me so much of my dear papa, who would never know how much his daughter had blossomed on the frontier.

"Thank you," I whispered.

He nodded.

And then belched.

Two days later the morning of the harvest dawned bright as a pearl. Unfortunately, one of our employees was not feeling the same way. The young man was groaning most disconsolately, clutching his stomach.

"I believe the poor boy had some bad clams," Mr. Swan said.

I had seen enough sick men in my time with Papa to know

that this young man was not going to be helping with the harvest. "We need another man," I said.

"Get Jehu," Keer-ukso suggested.

I found Jehu scrubbing his shirt in the stream by the Chinook village. It was in very poor condition, with a terrible tear on the sleeve. He was the only one of the men who didn't ask me to wash and mend his clothes.

"Can I take you up on your offer to help bring in the oysters for Mr. Swan and me?" I asked.

He looked up. "Sure."

"Aren't you even going to ask what I'm paying?"

"What are you paying?"

I told him.

"Fine," he said. "Let's go."

We went down to the bay and set out in our canoes for the oyster beds. A cool wind swept across the water, carrying with it a faintly fishy smell. I sat in Jehu's canoe and watched as he helped paddle us out to the beds.

It was low tide, so the oysters were easy to gather. The men simply stepped in the water and gathered them by hand into baskets, and then emptied the baskets in the canoe. As the day went on and the tide came in, we used long tongs to tug the oysters free.

Jehu and I worked companionably side by side. I held the basket while he fished out the oysters.

"What are you gonna do with your oyster money?" he asked, dropping an oyster into the basket.

"Buy new bedding for the cabin. Now that the men are gone, I'm going to burn every blanket in sight and finally rid the place of fleas."

"Better not let Brandywine in the cabin," he said, chuckling.

"Or Mr. Russell," I muttered under my breath.

"Look at this," Jehu said, opening an oyster that was already partially exposed.

He dug out something small with his knife and wiped it on his shirt. It was a small, if rather lopsided, pearl. But it was a lovely color, creamy as the ivory silk of a wedding dress.

"Here," he said, placing the small treasure in my hand, and closing my fingers over it.

"Oh," I said, reddening. It was all I could think of to say.

Time passed quickly, and the canoes soon groaned from the weight of the harvest. A great cheer went up at the end of the day when the last oysters were loaded onto the waiting schooner. Red Charley counted out the gold into my hand, minus his fee, and when he insisted on my shaking his hand, I did so before he could spit.

"Capital!" Mr. Swan said, as he and I and Jehu stood on the beach watching the schooner disappear with the setting sun. We were all alone, the men having gone back to their lodges. All at once a wave of exhaustion washed over me.

"You go home and have supper," Mr. Swan said solicitously. "I'll pay the men."

I agreed gratefully and pressed the gold into his hands.

"Come on, Jane," Jehu said. "I'll walk you back."

As we walked through the darkening woods to the cabin, I stumbled on a jutting root. A strong arm caught me by the elbow, and there was Jehu, looking down at me.

"You're not gonna puke on my boots, are you?" he asked with a wink.

I gave a little laugh, remembering how on the voyage from Philadelphia I had been terribly seasick all over his boots.

"No," I promised him. "Not this time, at least."

We continued on in silence, his hand on my elbow guiding me carefully. It was so comfortable simply to be with him and not have to speak.

When we reached the cabin, we lingered on the porch, stretching the moment out.

Finally, I said, "Well, I should certainly be able to afford some new bedding."

His eyes crinkled. "Bedding? You could buy a whole new bedroom with that money."

I sighed. "That would be something. I would love a bedroom of my own. No," I corrected myself, "I would love a house of my own. Some place where I wouldn't have to worry about strange men tramping through."

"What? You don't like Mr. Swan snoring in your ear every night?" he teased.

"Jehu."

"You should be proud of yourself," he said, pushing a curl off my forehead.

"For what?" I whispered unsteadily.

"For staying," he said simply.

As I fell asleep that night, I dreamed of all the things I would buy with my hard-earned funds—and also about a quiet sailor from Boston who let me puke on his boots.

The next morning when I woke up, Mr. Swan was not in the cabin. Indeed, it appeared his bunk had not even been slept in. It didn't take me long to discover where he had obviously spent the night: the grassy field by the Chinook lodges. Keer-ukso and Jehu were already there, standing over Mr. Swan. Someone had tossed a bucket of water on him. He was white-faced and wore a glazed expression.

"It seems that Mr. Swan got himself drunk and gambled away all your money," Jehu said in a disgusted voice.

"Mr. Swan—you didn't!" I gasped.

He looked shamefaced. "No," he clarified. "I gambled away all the money, and *then* got drunk."

"But we owe money to all those men!"

Mr. Swan shrugged helplessly. "I thought with all that money and a little luck, I could more than double our funds, but . . ." And here his voice trailed off.

"What are we to do? I don't have enough money left to pay them all. I invested nearly everything I had in hiring that second canoe. I can pay half of them, but what about the rest? All I have to my name is a bolt of fabric!" I shouted.

Jehu looked thoughtful, and then finally said, "I sure could use a new shirt."

"What do you mean?"

"You can pay me with a shirt. And I reckon the other men would appreciate a shirt, too."

"Do you think so?"

"Can't hurt to ask."

Keer-ukso explained the situation to the men we had hired. A hush fell over the group as they stared at us, annoyance plain on their faces. I couldn't bring myself to blame them. Finally, a young man called Kape stepped forward.

"Pie."

"Did he say pie?" I asked Keer-ukso quizzically.

Keer-ukso conferred with the young man and nodded. "One shirt and one pie each."

"But that's four shirts and four pies!"

Keer-ukso nodded ruefully.

"Seems word of your pies has spread," Jehu said with a wry smile.

It seemed it had.

CHAPTER FIVE
or,
A Lady at Last

November had arrived on the bay, bringing rain and a crisp wind, but I had barely noticed. I had spent the past week sewing and baking, and Jehu joked that my hair smelled like pie. I was still quite furious with Mr. Swan, though he went to great lengths to be solicitous to me. Our reputation in the oyster business was in ruins; I didn't know how we would ever hire help again.

One cool morning after finishing the final sleeve of the final shirt, I contemplated my blighted existence. I was full of frustration at the disagreeable men of Shoalwater Bay—Mr. Swan chief among them—and in that moment I resolved that I would have one small comfort for myself.

I would have a hot bath—or die trying.

I had not bathed in warm water since leaving Philadelphia almost a year ago, making do with sticky saltwater baths on the sea voyage, and then bathing in a freezing cold stream since arriving here.

After scouring the settlement high and low, I found a large empty wooden cask that had been sawn in half on the beach near where the schooners brought on fresh water. I dragged it around to the side of the cabin and rigged several blankets around it. Then I began the laborious process of heating water over the fire. Pot after pot of steaming water I brought carefully out of the cabin to fill the cask. Finally, when I was satisfied that the cask was full, I dashed back into the cabin in search of a clean towel and the small bar of lavender soap I had been hoarding.

As I rounded the corner, towel in hand, I heard the sound of men talking excitedly. I yanked back the blanket screen to see several bare-chested men huddled around the cask.

"What are you doing?" I demanded.

One of the men blushed slightly. "Our laundry, a course."

I ran over to the cask and peered inside. Filthy shirts swam in the now gray murky water.

"That was my bath!"

The men looked a little puzzled. One of them spoke up. "Since you said you wouldn't do our laundry no more, ma'am, we jest figured we'd have to do it ourselves. The water was jest sitting here, wasting away."

"It was not wasting away!"

I heard the familiar sound of spitting.

"Gal," Mr. Russell said, milking bucket in one hand and stool in the other. "Ya got to start milking Burton."

"These men just stole my bathwater!" I exploded at him. "And now you want me to milk your cow?"

45

Out of the corner of my eye, I saw the thieving men slink away.

Mr. Russell ignored my remark completely. "Gal, I can't be here all the time. If I go away, someone's got to take care of Burton."

I put my hands on my hips. While I had certainly performed more disgusting chores than milking a cow, I despised the beast almost as much as the man. Burton the cow had been responsible for eating my entire wardrobe when I'd first arrived on the bay.

I heard the cow mooing loudly in the distance, and Mr. Russell crooked his finger for me to follow him.

The cow was situated in a roofed stall not far from the cabin. The beast snapped her tail, as if she were as irritated as I at the thought of my milking her.

Mr. Russell patted the cow's rump gently, murmuring soothing words. "Now, gal, pull firmly, but go nice and easy. Bertie's real sensitive."

I stared at the cow dubiously.

"All right then, ya take a go at it, gal," Mr. Russell said. "Ain't nothing to be afeared of."

I drew myself up. "I am most certainly not afraid of a cow."

"Then go on."

His challenge hung on the air. I was Miss Jane Peck of Philadelphia. I was a proper young lady. I could organize a party for fifty. I could certainly milk a cow.

I sat down on the stool and gingerly positioned the bucket.

The cow swung her head around and glared at me. I took a deep breath and then I grabbed the teat firmly.

The cow bellowed and a spray of milk rained on my bosom. I let go of the teat and in the next moment I felt a distinct, sharp pain in my elbow as the cow kicked outward. The beast lunged at my head, snagging a swath of my hair in her teeth and tugging hard.

"Oww!"

I smacked the cow furiously and scrambled away, cradling my injured arm.

"Ya durn gal! I told ya to go nice and gentle!" Mr. Russell grizzled, hovering over the agitated cow.

"You told me to pull firmly!"

"Ya stupid useless gal! Ya scared my Bertie!"

The cow let out an indignant bellow.

"That beast tried to kill me!" I shot back. I held up my throbbing elbow.

I felt the swish of skirts brush against my back and looked up, startled.

A rosy-cheeked feminine face stared down at me with bemusement, dark tendrils escaping from a smooth bonnet. She looked to be about twenty, or perhaps twenty-one, and was as pretty as one of the drawings in *Godey's Lady's Book*. Mr. Swan was standing next to the woman, his flushed cheeks glowing with pleasure.

"This is Mrs. Frink, Jane. She and her husband have only just arrived, and so I brought her straight here. They traveled overland all the way from Ohio," Mr. Swan said, as if bestowing a present.

"How do you do, Miss Peck," the young woman said in a cultivated voice. She was tidily outfitted in a neat dress of yellow calico, a matching bonnet, and cream leather gloves. Although her clothes were not fancy dress, they were certainly of a nice cut. I was abruptly, painfully, aware that my skirts were covered with mud, my bodice soaked with cow's milk, and my hair tumbled down around my shoulders in a tangled heap.

"My, what unusual grass," she said, raising a curious arched eyebrow. "Is it peculiar to the region?"

"Grass?" Mr. Swan asked, rubbing his beard thoughtfully.

We followed her line of vision and saw the cow was chomping on something long and red, a baleful expression on her face.

I put a tentative hand up to my head.

And felt a patch of skin where hair should have been!

Mr. Russell snorted.

Mr. and Mrs. Frink had been married a little over a year. They had traveled in a wagon train, she informed me. She was eager to tell me about their travels.

Her husband had heard from a cousin that the area was booming, and as they had missed the gold rush, he was very eager that they try their luck on the bay. He had grand ideas of opening a hotel. Mrs. Frink was very fond of Mr. Frink, but men for all their good intentions were not as sensible as women, were they? After all, *she* had been the one to round up their horses when they'd spooked in Illinois, and it had been *her* negotiations with that disreputable ferryman that had gotten them across the river in Missouri, and then, of course, it had been *her* good suggestion to use the metal bits from the pickle barrel to mend the spare wheel when it had broken near the Snake River.

I learned all this as I changed into clean clothes behind the shabby blanket screen that served as a dressing area of sorts. Mrs. Frink had barely ceased speaking since entering the cabin. Mr. Swan had left her with me to provide a lady's hospitality while he went off to show her husband our burgeoning settlement, but Mrs. Frink had done most of the entertaining so far. I tried to attend her but was distracted by thoughts of how I must appear next to this new arrival. While my dresses were of serviceable calico, they were not as fashionable as Mrs. Frink's. I didn't even own a pair of gloves anymore, and my bonnet was quite sad-looking. Not to mention my shoes were ill-fitting boys' boots. I felt the same way I used to feel when Sally Biddle walked into a room.

Really, it all went back to Sally Biddle.

Picture a perfect girl with golden curls, a tiny waist, and all the best connections. Add to that an uncanny ability to make one cry with a single word, and that is Sally Biddle. Just thinking about her made all the misery come rushing back. How she used to say that my hair resembled a squirrel's nest, and whisper that I was plump, and belittle our house on Walnut Street, saying that it looked like a stable.

Perhaps the lone advantage of Shoalwater Bay was that it was situated a continent away from Sally Biddle in Philadelphia.

Mrs. Frink continued chatting from the other side of the

curtain. "'But Mr. Frink,' I said, 'I can't imagine that there will be much call for a hotel here on the frontier.'"

I fingered the newly bald patch on the side of my head. It was the size of a silver dollar. Blasted cow. There was no helping it. I tugged on my worn bonnet and came around the curtain in a determined fashion. I was not about to let this woman intimidate me the way Sally Biddle had in the past.

"What a charming dress!" Mrs. Frink exclaimed. "Such a lovely print."

"Thank you," I said cautiously. "I sewed it myself."

"How perfectly clever of you! Perhaps you would consider sewing a dress for me?"

I looked blankly at her immaculate dress.

"Oh," she said with a self-conscious laugh. "This is the only decent dress I have left. The rest were all quite ruined on the trail. This only survived because I packed it away."

I smiled at her. "I'd be happy to." I felt something tight in my chest loosen. She wasn't like Sally Biddle at all. She was more like what I imagined an older sister would be.

I poured her a cup of coffee and brought the sugar and milk to the table. It reminded me of Miss Hepplewhite's, the soothing ritual of pouring tea.

She clapped her hands happily. "You use tin, too, I see."

"Tin?"

"Tin cups, my dear. They're ever so practical." She lowered her voice. "I used our good china on the first week of the journey, but I grew so worried about breaking something that I packed it away and adopted the pioneer method of using tin plates and cups. It's ever so much more practical." She gave an exaggerated sigh. "And then, of course, our box of china fell out of our wagon during a stampede of buffalo somewhere back along the Platte River, so I have little choice now. I jumped out of the wagon after it and tried to shoo away the dratted animals with a broom, but I declare that they are the stupidest animals that ever lived, and the china was all smashed to bits except for the butter dish, which somehow lodged itself in a buffalo chip."

The image of proper Mrs. Frink brandishing a broom at stampeding buffalo in order to rescue her china was too much. I couldn't help it. I burst out laughing. I think I had not laughed since receiving word of Papa's death, and it felt so good, like a sneeze after being tickled.

Mrs. Frink looked affronted for a brief moment then giggled herself. "Mr. Frink was very vexed with me for jumping off the wagon," she confided. "'But Mr. Frink,' I said, 'good china is worth being trampled over!'"

"At least you rescued the butter dish," I said, wiping a tear away.

She nodded seriously and giggled again, "Yes, although I must confess, I have no desire to use it. I cannot seem to rid myself of the sight of it lodged in manure."

After we had finished our coffee, I offered to give Mrs. Frink a tour. At last, another lady! I had so many questions for her.

"It is so wonderful to be back in civilization!" Mrs. Frink declared happily.

I bit my tongue. The settlement was hardly civilization, unless you considered a pack of unwashed men who debated the finer points of chewing tobacco good company.

She turned to me. "I should very much like to meet the other ladies."

"Well," I hedged, as we stood on the porch surveying the cabins and tents that dotted the landscape. "I'm rather afraid that I am the only young lady present."

One elegant eyebrow raised slightly. "I see."

I rushed to reassure. "But the Chinook women are very kind, and quite a few speak English. They live that way," I said, pointing at the stream.

"Chinook? Do you mean Indians?"

I nodded.

"I see," she said again, an inscrutable expression on her face. "And who exactly lives in this cabin?" Mrs. Frink asked, wrinkling her small nose.

I twisted my hands. For all her stories of the trail, Mrs. Frink seemed a very proper sort of lady. Her gloves were spotless. I imagined she would be horrified to learn that I had been living unchaperoned in a cabin with assorted men these many past months. It would be utterly inappropriate behavior for a respectable young lady under ordinary circumstances.

I swallowed hard. "Well, myself, and Mr. Russell, and Mr. Swan, and sometimes Keer-ukso, and, and . . . and sometimes whatever men are passing through," I finished in an awkward rush.

She eyed the cabin coolly. "My, but what a luxury to have a proper roof over one's head," she said with real longing.

My mouth fell open.

"I have been sleeping under the stars or in our wagon for the past six months. The canvas covering our wagon is in a very sad state, I fear."

I was taken aback by her candor.

"Although," she said, her voice softening, "I must confess to growing accustomed to falling asleep with stars over my head. The most beautiful sight I have ever seen was when I lay on the plains at night, the starry sky stretching above us like a quilt." She blinked and laughed. "Of course, I was worried to death that Indians would steal our horses."

"Did they?"

"Once, but they let us buy them back." She eyed the well-worn trail leading away from the cabin. "Shall we meet your neighbors?"

"Of course," I said. "Right this way."

"So do you think, Miss Peck, that there will be much call for a hotel out here?" she asked in a serious voice, as if she truly valued my opinion.

"There are many men around here who would be happy for a proper bed and a cooked meal. A hotel might be quite popular, actually. I imagine I'd be the first to stay there. Especially if there were a bathtub."

She laughed, a bright tinkly laugh that made me smile. "We are going to be such great friends, Miss Peck. I just know it."

We followed the stream down past a small, neat building with a cedar plank roof. A cross jutted from the ceiling.

"That is Father Joseph's chapel. He's a French Catholic missionary. He came on the same boat I did."

"Is he having much success spreading the faith?"

"I'm afraid not," I said.

"Poor man." She grinned at me impishly. "But then again, who likes to be told what to do, even by a man of the cloth?"

We rounded a bend in the trail and entered the large grassy clearing where the huge cedar lodges of Chief Toke's village were clustered.

"Are those the Indians?" Mrs. Frink asked.

I looked about. Nearby, chopping a pile of firewood with axes, was a group of the men I had hired to harvest the oysters, all wearing identical shirts.

"Well, yes," I said.

"How very interesting," she said. "I thought they'd be more like the Indians on the trail. But here they are, all dressed up like us!"

Sootie came running straight at me, chattering happily, and dragging her doll.

"Boston Jane! Boston Jane!" Sootie yelled. "Is this your sister? She looks just like you, except your hair is prettier. But I like her dress better."

Mrs. Frink and I looked at each other in embarrassment.

54

"Sootie," I said, trying to slow the rush of words. "This is Mrs. Frink."

"What a charming child!" Mrs. Frink exclaimed. "Is that a doll you have there?"

Sootie held out her doll for inspection. "Boston Jane made my dolly a new dress," she informed her importantly.

"And it's quite a lovely dress, too," Mrs. Frink complimented, and I smiled at the woman for her kindness.

"Sootie is Chief Toke's daughter," I said. "He is the chief, or *tyee*, of this village."

"A chief?" Mrs. Frink said, impressed.

"That's right!" Sootie said proudly. "Because he is the most rich."

"Sootie, do you know where your father is?" I asked.

She pressed her lips together for a minute and then said, "He is with Mr. Russell and Mr. Swan and some other man. I don't like Mr. Russell very much," she informed Mrs. Frink. "And he has a cow that keeps us up all night sometimes."

"Was that the gentleman with whom you were milking the cow when I arrived?" Mrs. Frink asked.

"Yes. He was the first pioneer to come here." I was preparing to launch into an explanation of Mr. Russell's business and character when Mr. Swan, Mr. Russell, and a man who I supposed must be Mr. Frink came sauntering over to where we stood.

"Ah, Jane, there you are. Capital," Mr. Swan announced.

"Miss Peck has been very kindly giving me a tour," Mrs.

Frink said, patting the man on his arm. "Miss Peck, may I introduce my husband, Mr. Frink?"

Mr. Frink, who in distinct contrast to his wife, looked like he had just spent six months on the trail in his worn boots and dirty shirt, shook my hand.

Mrs. Frink turned her attention to Mr. Russell. "Miss Peck tells me you were the first pioneer in the area, Mr. Russell."

"First but not last, ma'am. We're real pleased to have you here." To my utter astonishment, Mr. Russell removed his hat and smoothed back his hair. "We don't get too many ladies out this way."

What about me? I was a lady! He had never once, in all my time on Shoalwater Bay, removed his hat because of my presence!

"We're very happy to be here," Mrs. Frink replied with a gay smile.

"That's a real pretty dress you're wearing, if you don't mind my saying so," Mr. Russell added, blushing furiously.

"Why, Miss Peck, you didn't tell me what a charming man Mr. Russell was," Mrs. Frink said with a wide smile, extending her arm to him.

Mr. Russell took it gallantly and led her toward the cabin.

All I could do was stare.

CHAPTER SIX
or,
The Charming Mrs. Frink

All at once, the men of Shoalwater Bay found it very important to bathe and wash and generally look presentable.

They cut their hair. They scrubbed their hands. They brushed their teeth. Even Mr. Russell attempted to shave his straggly beard in order to look more respectable, but he succeeded only in carving his face.

They vied to spend a moment in Mrs. Frink's presence. With a simple smile, she had a cabin built. With a downward sweep of her lashes, she had acquired an outhouse. With an upward turn of her lips, her garden was dug.

It was perfectly astonishing. It was almost as if she were the first lady to arrive on the bay, when I had been here for months and months! The men had never treated me the way they did Mrs. Frink—with a mix of awe and respect and admiration.

After much worry on my part, I invited the Frinks to supper one late-November day. They had taken up residence in their new cabin, which was situated on a lovely patch of land with a view of the bay. And which, I might add, the men of the settlement had built without having to be bribed with whiskey.

I spent two days carefully planning the menu. I had learned how to cook while on Shoalwater Bay, but while I regularly cooked for men, I had never cooked for another lady. I was well aware that the men ate anything I put before them, especially Mr. Russell, but I expected that Mrs. Frink would have a more refined palate.

In the end I settled on roast chicken, biscuits and gravy, and a pie for dessert. Not that it mattered, for the men were far too busy paying attention to Mrs. Frink to compliment me on the excellent meal I had prepared. All they could do was listen to Mrs. Frink's witty stories of her travels west, and by the time I started clearing dishes, the men were hanging on her every word. These men, who belched and spat at every opportunity, somehow managed to contain their belches and not spit once during the entire meal.

Mrs. Frink was relating a story in which she had stayed up all night to watch the campsite because the men on the wagon train were so exhausted. Her husband, whom I had yet to hear speak, sat quietly at her side, smoking his pipe.

"My poor Mr. Frink," Mrs. Frink said, patting her husband's hand, "had worked the work of four men. Why, he single-handedly pulled our wagon out of a ditch as deep as I am tall! What else could I do but let the perfect man sleep?"

Mr. Frink just puffed on his pipe.

"Then what happened?" Mr. Russell asked anxiously, gray

whiskers twitching. He had procured a clean shirt from some-where, although the sleeve already had a gravy stain from where he'd used it as his napkin.

"Yes, well, that was the time I shot the coyote, of course."

"You can shoot?" I asked, aghast. Not only was she a lady, but she could shoot?

She inclined her head slightly. "I'm a very good shot, Miss Peck. Mr. Frink taught me how to shoot."

The men nodded admiringly.

I remembered with some embarrassment my lone attempt at wielding a rifle. A cougar had been sneaking into the encamp-ment, and I had fired at it and missed. Still, at least it had run off.

Mr. Russell leaned forward, intent on capturing every word that tripped off her tongue.

"You see, a coyote snuck into camp and tried to make away with our best piece of bacon. Well, I fired right at the scamp's tail, and it went yelping off into the night—and that was the last we saw of that coyote!" She gave a little laugh. "That was also the last time I left the bacon out."

The men clapped.

I began clearing away the plates, feeling a little like a maid. Jehu quietly stood up and began gathering plates as well.

"Oh, do sit down, Mr. Scudder. I shall help, Jane," Mrs. Frink offered grandly, standing. There was a clatter as, all at once, chairs were shoved back and Mr. Russell, Mr. Swan, Mr. Frink, and Keer-ukso stood. "Miss Peck," Mrs. Frink tittered, "you are so fortunate to be surrounded by so many gentlemen."

The men blushed.

I shot them all a dark look. Really, no one ever bothered to stand when I got up from the table. I furiously began to carve the pie I had made earlier that day. Mrs. Frink appeared with a covered dish in her hand.

"I brought my famous crumble cake. Mr. Frink just adores my crumble cake," she confided. "My clever husband was so smart to bring that iron stove in the wagon." I just stared at the cake.

"You've been kindness itself, cooking supper for all of us," she continued, pressing my hand. "Really. It was the least I could do."

I didn't want to appear ungracious. "Well, I suppose we could serve both."

Mrs. Frink announced, "For dessert there is a choice of Miss Peck's pie or my crumble cake."

"I'll take the crumble cake," Mr. Russell said quickly.

"For me as well," Mr. Swan said with a broad smile.

Mr. Frink merely nodded in assent. I was beginning to wonder if the man had a tongue in his head.

Jehu's eyes rested on my face. "I'll have a piece of pie. Jane makes wonderful pie."

Mrs. Frink turned to Keer-ukso. There was a moment of uncomfortable silence and then Keer-ukso said, a little reluctantly, "Pie, too."

I smiled at him gratefully.

Mr. Russell took a hearty bite of Mrs. Frink's crumble cake and closed his eyes in delight. "This here's the best thing I've ever tasted," he said with true fervor, devouring his slice of crumble cake in two quick bites and then holding out his plate for a second helping. "I'd be much obliged if you'd cut me another piece, ma'am."

Mrs. Frink bestowed a radiant smile upon him and carved off another piece of cake.

"Capital cake, my dear woman. Simply marvelous," Mr. Swan declared in his effusive way, a crumb clinging to his beard. He held out his empty plate to Mrs. Frink for another piece as well.

Keer-ukso looked with real longing at the famous crumble cake, his pie untouched.

What about my pie? I wanted to shout. Until now, my pie had been the best thing on Shoalwater Bay. All the men said so!

Mrs. Frink was perfect! She had the manners of Miss Hepplewhite, and she could shoot a gun like a man and bake a cake better than me! Why, she even spoke perfect French.

"Madame Frink has read *Manon Lescaut* in the original," Father Joseph had told me in an impressed voice. Whatever that was!

I was terrible at languages and had barely learned how to say "May I have a fresh napkin?" during my Conversational French lessons at Miss Hepplewhite's Young Ladies Academy.

I had longed for female companionship, but now that another lady had arrived, I rather wished she'd go back to Ohio.

Even Brandywine, the useless beast, followed her around. He shamelessly flipped on his back to get her to rub his plump belly.

Jehu alone seemed immune to her charm.

"Do you like Mrs. Frink?" I asked Keer-ukso the next day as

we sat on the beach in the early morning light. The sun was hiding behind a thick gray sky, and the day perfectly reflected my bad mood.

He shrugged.

"Do you know that Mr. Russell offered to build her a chimney? That man never even offered to put up a tent for me! And now he's going to build her a chimney?"

"Chimney is no good," Keer-ukso said. "Swan's chimney fell down."

Keer-ukso had a very poor opinion of chimneys on all account of Mr. Swan's chimney crashing down during a thunderstorm and almost killing us all.

"Yes, but that's not the point. The point is she has all the men scurrying around to help her and do things for her when they would never do anything for me!"

Keer-ukso looked affronted. "I help Boston Jane."

"Yes, I didn't mean you. I meant the others."

He narrowed his eyes at me. "You have *sick tumtum*."

Sick tumtum meant jealous.

"No, I'm not jealous," I hedged. "Well, maybe I am, but only a little. It's just that, that," I blustered, "I'm a lady, too, but nobody ever treats me like her. Nobody ever built me an outhouse!" I finished in a huff.

Keer-ukso just shook his head and said, *"Sick tumtum."*

Later that day as I was sitting on a log on the beach trying to stitch some ribbon onto one of my skirts, I pricked my finger and realized that I would never sew a skirt as fashionable as Mrs.

Frink's. No matter how hard I tried, I would never be as good as her. It was almost as if I were back in Philadelphia with Sally Biddle. Except that Mrs. Frink was worse than Sally Biddle, because she was so nice.

Mr. Swan came tramping over, stick in hand. His cheeks were ruddy from the crisp weather.

"Hello, my dear," Mr. Swan said. "Capital day!"

It was gray and drizzly as usual.

"Hmmph," I said.

"Have you seen Mrs. Frink?" he asked cheerfully.

"No."

"Charming woman, Mrs. Frink. Simply charming!" Mr. Swan mused.

"Oh, I know. It's perfectly plain that the entire world thinks she's charming," I said, a bitter edge to my voice.

He looked startled. "My dear?"

I shook my head and sighed.

Mr. Swan patted my hand. "We are all very fond of you, my dear."

They were all very fond of me? But they adored Mrs. Frink and I was plainly not in the same class as her.

"I must be off." Mr. Swan cleared his throat importantly. "Mrs. Frink has asked my opinion on the architectural plans for the hotel, and I have some interesting ideas." He paused. "Would you like to join me?"

I shook my head.

It was so vexing. Mr. Swan was *my* friend, *my* business

partner. I wanted to ask why couldn't he have some interesting ideas about our oyster business, but instead I simply stared at the bay.

"Ah well, I shall see you later then, my dear," Mr. Swan said awkwardly, and walked away.

I spent the rest of the afternoon stalking up and down the beach. The men could fix their own supper for once, I thought angrily, as I walked off my frustration. It would do them good to see how much work I did. They didn't appreciate me. Why, they barely remembered to thank me! Not to mention, no one ever offered to help clear the table, except, of course, Jehu.

The sun had sunk behind the mountains when I finally returned to the cabin. I fully expected to be met by a group of angry, hungry men, but instead all that greeted me was silence. The cabin was dark, and the fire had been allowed to burn out. Where had everyone gone?

And then I heard Brandywine barking. I followed the sound of his barking down the path that led to the Frinks' cabin. The dog was whining piteously at the door to be let in. Was something wrong? I knocked, and after a moment the door opened.

"Why hello, Miss Peck!" Mrs. Frink exclaimed in delight.

I looked past her shoulder, my eyes widening in surprise. Sitting around a table that bore the remains of a roast chicken supper with biscuits and gravy—and mashed potatoes!—were all the men. Mr. Swan was happily tucking away a big piece of Mrs. Frink's crumble cake, the crumbs clinging to his beard.

"Do join us, Miss Peck," Mrs. Frink said graciously, stepping aside, but all I could do was stand there and stare at them. "We were just beginning to worry about you."

"Jane," Jehu said, pushing back his chair.

But I didn't wait to speak to him. I turned and ran off into the black night, knowing that I could disappear tomorrow and no one would miss me.

No one at all.

The next morning Mrs. Frink appeared in my doorway.

"Miss Peck," she began carefully, "would you care to come over to our cabin and have tea this afternoon?"

I wanted to say no, but all those years at Miss Hepplewhite's Young Ladies Academy stopped me, and I found myself saying yes and thanking her for the invitation.

In short order, Mrs. Frink and I were sitting at her table across from each other. Before us sat tin cups of tea poured by her hand and flavored perfectly with milk and sugar. I could not have poured a better cup of tea myself.

Mrs. Frink smiled brightly. "So tell me, Miss Peck. What have you been doing with yourself these last few months? One has so much free time without social obligations, don't you agree? That was one thing I did not miss on the trail, I confess," and here she gave a little laugh.

I wanted to say that I'd been spending all my free time surviving, not to mention washing every shirt in the territory several times. Instead, I said, "I rather miss calling on acquaintances."

Mrs. Frink worried her lip and swallowed. "Mr. Swan says that you're quite a talented watercolorist."

"I'm afraid that Mr. Swan was no doubt drunk when he said so."

"Yes, well, I'd love to see your work sometime." She tittered nervously. "So I may judge for myself." Mrs. Frink's gaze settled on my hair. "And you must come over another time and let me do something with your hair. I have a simply wonderful collection of combs, and I'm certain we could make a very fashionable arrangement," she said eagerly.

My hand flew to my head automatically. I was wearing a bonnet to hide the bald patch, but I knew those unruly stray curls that Sally Biddle used to tease me about were escaping everywhere. "No, thank you," I said coldly, and had the satisfaction of seeing Mrs. Frink's face fall.

She pushed a plate of shortbread over to me. "Please have some shortbread, although it's not nearly as delightful as your pie. You must please give me the receipt for that pie," Mrs. Frink said in a strained voice.

She wanted the receipt so that she could make it for the men!

I stood up, knocking my chair back. "That receipt is a family secret."

Mrs. Frink wrung her hands. "Miss Peck, please forgive me. This is not what I had intended. This is going very badly indeed. Please, let us be friends. I know how hard it has been with you, and your unfortunate history with Mr. Baldt, and—"

I didn't want this woman's pity! "I do not appreciate your gossiping about me behind my back," I said tightly. "Please excuse me. I find that I have lost my appetite."

And with that, I walked quickly from the cabin.

Later that afternoon as I was cutting out biscuits for supper, the door banged open.

"I don't know where Mrs. Frink is," I said irritably, not looking up.

"Wasn't looking for Mrs. Frink," Jehu said dryly. "I was looking for you."

"I'm making supper," I said in a dogged voice.

And then without any explanation, he grabbed my hand and tugged me out the door.

"Jehu," I protested.

He just shook his head, and held my hand more tightly with his warm one. He led me along the curving beach in the opposite direction from where the Frinks were constructing their hotel, and the farther we walked away from the encampment and Mrs. Frink's influence, the calmer I felt. The wind whipping off the water cooled my temper.

"Where are we going?" I asked.

"You'll see," he said mysteriously.

We rounded a bend along the bay, and there it was: a rich, green vista, mountains rising high above, sheltering the land like a cove. He led me up a rocky cliff to stand on the edge.

"What do you think?" he asked. He swept his hand in front of

67

him, at the warm afternoon light dancing across the bay. Water stretched out in all directions, and the sound of soft waves lapping against the shore was comforting, like Brandywine's snore. A sparkling stream ran down one side of the cliff.

It was perfect, perhaps the most perfect spot on the bay.

"It's lovely."

He grinned, the scar in his cheek crinkling. "I thought so," he said in a very self-satisfied voice.

I peered over the edge of the cliff. "It is a bit high."

He raised a disbelieving eyebrow. "You're afraid of heights?"

I nodded. "Although, when I was a little girl, my playmate Jebediah Parker and I used to run along the rooftops, spitting at men passing far below."

"You? Spit?" he asked, a look of pure astonishment on his face.

"I was very good at spitting. There were men who walked around Philadelphia all day long who never even knew that they had great gobs of spit on their hats." I couldn't help it; I giggled.

Jehu roared in laughter, the sound goading me into remembrance.

"We were fearless, just running along the roofs. It was a whole different world."

"So when did you become afraid of heights, then?" he asked, puzzled.

"One spring day a gentleman we spat on was so furious that he chased us halfway across Philadelphia. And just when we thought we'd escaped him, he appeared on the roof, brandishing a cane at us. I was so startled that I lost my balance and slipped."

Jehu's expression silently encouraged me to continue.

"I fell, but I grabbed onto the ledge, and just hung on. The man came over and hauled me up, but only after letting me dangle there for what seemed like forever, wondering whether or not I was going to fall to my death."

I swallowed hard, remembering the sheer terror of hovering above the street, my fingers grappling the loose bricks. "After he finally pulled me up, he took one look at my white face and said in a satisfied voice, 'I don't think you'll be spitting on hats anymore.'"

Jehu whistled through his teeth.

"And he was right," I said with a weak smile.

"Oh, Jane," Jehu said, taking my shoulders in his hands and looking at me, his eyes so clear with . . . what? Worry for the little girl who had once been fearless? But it didn't matter, because all at once I remembered the feel of his lips against mine as we danced beneath a starry sky mere months ago. He had held me then, too, his hands warm about my waist, and we were spinning, spinning, spinning—

"I've put in a claim," he said abruptly.

"Oh," I said.

"I was thinking I'd build a house right here. I know you like to look at the bay."

I looked into the eyes of this quiet, sturdy, dependable man, and now saw his desire to please me so clearly on his tanned face.

"It's going to have a balcony on the water." He leaned into me, his arms at my waist now, his body warm. "And there'll be steps leading to the beach." He leaned even closer, his breath tickling my ear. "And there's a grove of trees with a slope just on the edge of the property line."

The wind seemed to blow gently, like a sigh, humming between us. And to think that I had once turned him away because of William Baldt, a man who wanted to marry me to get more land!

"Jehu," I said, tugging his head down to mine.

"And on the other side of that," he breathed, his cheek brushing against mine, his unshaven face tickling like so many butterfly wings, "there's another plot of land that I'd like to put in a claim for."

Something cold settled in my chest.

"Another claim," I said in a dull voice, remembering William's schemes.

"Yes, you see I have plans to—"

But I wasn't listening anymore. I suddenly knew why he'd brought me here. He wanted to marry me to get more land, just like William Baldt.

For *land*. Not for *me*!

I yanked away from the circle of his arms. "You're despicable!"

"I want—"

"Oh, I know exactly what you want," I bit out furiously.

Jehu stared at me, a bewildered expression on his face.

"Boston Jane!"

I turned to the voice, grateful for the distraction. Sootie was running toward us, crying.

Jehu dropped my hand, his jaw muscles working.

"Boston Jane," Sootie cried anxiously, her small face streaked with tears. The little girl flung herself into my arms and began sobbing in earnest. I held her tight, refusing to meet Jehu's eyes. After a moment, I set her away gently.

"What's the matter, sweetheart?"

She thrust a small bundle into my hands. It was her clam doll, or what was left of it anyway.

"Brandywine ate dolly!" Sootie cried, and burst into tears again.

"Oh dear," I said.

"Jane," Jehu said in a low voice.

I ignored him and gave Sootie a hug, glaring over her shoulder at him.

He flung up his hands and stalked away.

CHAPTER SEVEN
or,
An Unexpected Guest

I woke to cool, crisp weather and the sound of horses neighing like fretful children.

November had slipped away, and December had arrived like an unexpected guest, cold and blustery and demanding attention. Outside the cabin I heard the sound of horses and wondered who it might be. Horses were in short supply on the bay. I quickly pulled my dress on over my head, not bothering to brush my tangled locks. By now my bald patch was covered with a thin, stubby layer of hair. I grabbed up my cape and went out to the porch.

He looked much the same as when I'd first met him. Bright blond hair and chiseled chin. Pale gray eyes. An impossibly straight nose.

"William," I said stiffly to my former betrothed.

"Jane," he replied uncomfortably.

He had been my father's apprentice back in Philadelphia,

and he had lodged with us in our house on Walnut Street. The images flashed through my mind. Papa and William and I laughing at the supper table. The three of us sitting in the parlor in front of the cheery fire. Papa and William debating medical treatments. He was the only one in the entire territory who would ever remember Papa the way I did—strong, robust, laughing—and alive. I felt a rush of grief so strong that the only thing I could do was stand there and look at him.

"Papa's dead," I finally blurted.

Something in his face softened. "I heard, Jane. Mr. Swan told me. I'm very sorry. He was a fine man. I admired him greatly."

He took a step toward me, taking hold of my hands, bending his head, and the smell of him, so near, so wrapped up in my memories of Philadelphia and Papa, caused something in me to loosen, something I had been holding tight next to my heart for weeks now. Without warning, tears ran down my face, hot with held-in pain and aching sorrow and a thousand regrets.

"Oh, Jane," he said softly, his voice so familiar.

I don't know how long we stood there on the porch with me weeping into his scratchy wool shirt. All I know is that when I heard Mr. Russell's voice I stepped quickly away.

"Gal?" Mr. Russell asked, eyeing William darkly.

I wiped my eyes quickly, sniffling.

Mr. Swan was rushing toward us across the clearing, his face anxious. "Oh, my dear, I neglected to tell you that William was arriving—" he began hurriedly.

"As you can see, I've discovered him myself," I said, looking at William and taking in for the first time the two other men on horses behind him. They looked travel worn and tired. By the way one of the horses was pawing the ground, it seemed that the animals were as fatigued as the men.

"What exactly are you doing here?" I asked William, abruptly remembering that this man was responsible for my being in this blasted wilderness.

"Confidential business for the governor," William said shortly. His eyes lingered on my bald patch, and I felt his disapproval as clearly as I had all those years ago when I was a little girl running around with stained aprons and tangled hair.

"Oh yes, well, harrumph," Mr. Swan interrupted, shifting on his feet, shooting an urgent plea for help to Mr. Russell. "Perhaps, William, you and your men might want to let your horses rest for a bit?"

Mr. Russell jerked his head and said, "Thar's a stream yonder where ya can water yer animals."

William nodded, fatigue evident in his eyes. "We need some sleep. We've been riding hard for three days now." He looked pointedly at Mr. Russell's cabin.

If William thought that he was going to stay in this cabin, he was most mistaken.

As if reading my thoughts, Mr. Swan spoke clearly. "I do believe I can lend you and your men some very comfortable tents."

William just grunted. Without a backward glance he took

the reins of his horse and headed toward the stream, his men following him. When he was out of sight, I whirled on Mr. Swan.

"How could you not tell me he was coming?"

Mr. Swan looked apologetic. "My dear girl, I truly wish I'd warned you. It's just that I was speaking with Toke and we lost track of the time and—"

"Mr. Swan!" I stamped my foot. "What is he doing here?"

"Yes. Well. As you know, Jane, William is the governor's man. And the governor has called for a meeting—a rendezvous, really—of all the tribes in this part of the territory. William will be escorting us to the rendezvous along with representatives of the tribe. Mr. Russell and I are going along to translate."

"When do you leave?"

"Tomorrow morning."

So this was why Mr. Russell wanted me to learn how to milk Burton the cow.

"Now my dear, it would be lovely if you could prepare a special supper since William is here."

"Mr. Swan, how can you even ask that?" I demanded. Cook supper for the lout who had dragged me west and married another woman?

Mr. Swan was wringing his hands anxiously. "I know that this is very awkward, but William has the governor's ear, and what he decides could influence the fate of our little community."

By which he meant that William could force Keer-ukso, and Sootie, and Chief Toke, and all the Chinook onto a reservation, and then where would we be? I thought of Sootie, and schooled myself. After all, it was just one meal.

"Very well," I mumbled.

"Capital, capital," Mr. Swan said, and started to walk away. He paused, turning. "I don't suppose you'd make a pie?"

I just glared at him.

When William had lived with Papa and me at our house on Walnut Street, we had employed help to cook our supper and wait on us. In Mr. Russell's cabin I had no help unless you considered Brandywine, although the only service he provided was eating whatever scraps fell to the floor.

The men crowded around the sawbuck table: Mr. Swan, Mr. Russell, Chief Toke, Keer-ukso, Jehu, Father Joseph, and William. I had made up plates for the other two men in William's party, and they were eating on the porch.

Jehu's attendance rather surprised me. I had not spoken with him for several days—not since our confrontation on the cliff—but he had showed up at the cabin with Keer-ukso and Chief Toke. And he seemed to be spending a great deal of time quietly studying William.

The raucous sounds of eating punctuated by the occasional belch filled the cabin as the men dug into their biscuits and gravy. The fire flickered warmly and I took my own plate to the table, squeezing in next to Father Joseph and across from Jehu.

William sat at the head of the table. "This is very good, Jane," he said. "I didn't know you could cook."

"There's rather a lot you don't know about me," I said in a low voice.

I expected him to snipe back at me but he merely laughed, a condescending sort of laugh. I bit my tongue and stared down at my plate. Under the table I felt a knee brush against mine, and I looked up to see Jehu's stoic face.

"So tell me, William, what are the governor's intentions?" Mr. Swan asked, flecks of gravy in his beard.

"I am recommending to the governor that the Indians in this part of the territory be placed on a reservation," he said importantly. He didn't seem to care that Chief Toke was sitting right in front of him.

Mr. Swan struggled to finish chewing, and then, as if carefully choosing his words, said, "Well, William, I think you will find some opposition to that course of action."

"What do you mean, 'opposition'?" William asked guardedly. His hair shone in the firelight like a golden flame. "From whom?"

"From me, for a start," Mr. Russell said. He looked appraisingly around the table. "I been here a sight longer than all of ya, and when I first got here I wouldn't have survived without the Indians. And now we depend on 'em. Who do ya think cuts the wood, and helps with the oystering and such? Thar ain't no point in moving 'em to a reservation. We won't have any men." He chewed a lump of tobacco and spit it on the floor. "'Sides, we ain't got no troubles. We live fine together. Real peaceful. We get more trouble from the bears if ya ask me, always sneaking in and stealing our salmon."

Nervous laughter punctuated the silence.

"Your position is rather unfortunately in conflict with the government's policy. There has been trouble elsewhere. The savages are unpredictable. It is our duty to protect you—from yourself, if necessary," William added.

Mr. Russell's eyes flicked over to William. "Don't much care for the government's opinion of things. That's why I come out here in the first place."

Father Joseph cleared his throat. "Monsieur Baldt, these Indians feel very strongly about living close to their ancestors' graves."

"They're superstitious, the lot of them," William said dismissively.

"Monsieur, they are no different than we are. Do we not wish to live near the resting places of our loved ones?"

Chief Toke's eyes met mine from across the table, and I swear he winked at me. Winked!

"Boston William," Chief Toke said in good, clear English, startling William. "You are foolish, but all young men are foolish. You should marry older woman. She make you wiser."

"I already have a wife, thank you," William said coldly, completely missing Chief Toke's point. But no one else did.

Clearly, trying to tell William that the Chinooks were our friends would fall on deaf ears, so I took a more practical approach.

"William, Mr. Russell is right. Who shall help us with the oyster harvest?" I asked. "We are all very much dependent on the goodwill and advice of Toke's people."

"Miss Peck," William said in a formal voice, his face going dark. "Obviously, your education was for naught. You've never learned that politics and matters of state are not affairs for a lady. Perhaps you ought to concern yourself with more suitable pursuits"—he shot a scathing look at my bald patch—"such as your hair."

Jehu, who had been silent the whole meal, turned to Keer-ukso and murmured, *"Yaka kahkwa pelton."*

Keer-ukso nodded firmly, his eyes all seriousness. *"Nowitka. Kahkwa hoolhool."*

Mr. Swan's eyes flew wide open in something approaching dismay, but Mr. Russell just puffed on his pipe. Chief Toke nodded his head silently, as if in agreement.

"You speak the Jargon?" I asked Jehu, rather surprised.

He shrugged.

William leaned forward, a curl to his lip, and addressed Jehu in a clipped voice. "And what, good sir, did you say?"

"You're an Indian agent and you don't speak the Jargon?" Jehu asked, his Boston accent a stark contrast to William's cultivated Philadelphia accent.

"I have no need to learn such gibberish," he said coldly. "Now, what did you say? And I caution you, sir, I am the governor's man in the territory."

His threat hung on the air.

Jehu stared at him calmly.

The whole room had gone whisper quiet as we watched the two men stare each other down. Tension was thick in the air, and the room, which had mere moments ago seemed warm and welcoming, suddenly felt charged. I had no idea what Jehu had said to Keer-ukso, but I had a suspicion it wasn't very complimentary. William was right about one thing: he was the governor's man, and he could harm both Jehu and Toke's people. It was a dangerous situation. I leaped up and went to a shelf where I had put the pie.

"Would anyone care for pie?" I asked, holding out the tin pan, a forced smile on my face.

"What did you say?" William hissed at Jehu.

Jehu merely stretched. He turned to me, and there was a twinkle in his eye. "Just that I was hoping Jane would be serving pie for dessert."

I breathed out in relief.

"And will you look at this," he said, holding out his plate, his eyes wide with mischief. "It seems she is."

The men were up bright and early the next morning. Mr. Swan was bustling about the cabin in a very determined sort of way, packing a sack with biscuits from the previous evening and raiding any food in plain sight.

"When will you be back?" I pushed myself up on my elbows sleepily.

He pulled his wool blanket off his bunk, crumpled it into a ball, and shoved this also into his sack. Were these men not capable of folding anything? "Perhaps two weeks, maybe three, my dear. I suppose it depends on how the negotiations go. We are not due at the rendezvous until next week. The journey itself shall take only a few days by canoe, but we are going to pick up representatives from other tribes, and no doubt we shall visit with them for a time. I am looking forward to seeing other parts of this territory." He waved his precious diary at me. "It shall be an adventure!"

He strode to the door and I followed him onto the porch, tugging a blanket around my shoulders. It was barely light out, but William and his men, as well as Mr. Russell and Chief Toke, were already assembled in a little group in the clearing.

"I see His Highness is leaving," a voice at my side said.

It was Jehu, a pack slung over his shoulder, his blue eyes fierce, one thick black curl flopped heartstoppingly over his forehead.

"You were gonna marry that cussed fool?" he asked, shaking his head, disgust in his voice.

I tugged my blanket tighter around me, forcing myself to remember that he was no better than William.

"At least I'm becoming a more skillful judge of character," I said.

"Jane," he said, "you've got the wrong idea—"

"On the contrary, I understand your intentions perfectly."

He rubbed his hair in frustration. "Look, I'm heading over to M'Carty's homestead. He broke his leg and his roof's only half done, and winter's on the way. Keer-ukso and I are going to lend a hand. We'll probably get our meals over there."

"Your comings and goings are no concern of mine, Mr. Scudder."

"You're stubborner than a mule," Jehu retorted, and then stomped away before I could get another word in.

"Who is he, your admirer?"

I turned to see William perched on his horse. The way he held himself—with such arrogance and self-possession—infuriated me.

"He's a better man than you'll ever be," I said.

"My, you've acquired quite a tongue," William said. His next words were like a blow. "Then again, I imagine it's from living unchaperoned on the frontier."

"You're the reason I'm here, you, you—"

Mr. Swan came bounding over. "Yoo-hoo, William!"

"Cussed fool!" I finished furiously.

"Well, my dear, we really must go!" Mr. Swan interrupted loudly, looking desperately between us. He donned a jaunty-looking cap. "Why don't you and your men start out, William? Mr. Russell and Chief Toke and I shall be along in a minute."

William turned his horse and urged it forward without a backward glance.

"He's horrible," I muttered, rubbing my stubby patch of hair.

Mr. Swan gave me a strained smile. "It is a very big territory, my dear. I'm sure you won't have to see him often. And now we must be going."

"You're leaving me all alone again?"

Mr. Swan had the good grace to look uncomfortable. The last time he had gone off with Mr. Russell and Chief Toke there had been a smallpox outbreak. "Well, my dear," he hedged, "you won't be alone. Mr. and Mrs. Frink are within shouting distance."

I stared at the porch floor, focusing on an ant winding its way along the board.

Mr. Swan laid a gentle hand on my shoulder. "Is something bothering you, Jane? Really, I'm sure you'll be fine with Mrs. Frink here."

Was something bothering me? *Yes!* I wanted to shout. I'm tired of blasted Mrs. Frink. I'm tired of everyone ignoring me and taking me for granted and treating me like a maid.

I'm tired of being so utterly alone.

Instead I merely mumbled, "No." I refused to meet his eyes. I stared down stubbornly at the floor.

"Good girl. If you need anything, just ask—"

"The Frinks," I finished in a dull voice.

"Don't forget to milk Burton," Mr. Russell called, spitting loudly. "Or she'll bust."

I hoped she did just that.

Because I had every intention of forgetting to milk the beast.

CHAPTER EIGHT
or,
A Gentleman Arrives on the Bay

The sound of Burton's mooing woke me with a start.

From the glimmer in the sky it must have been just after dawn. The men had only been gone for a day. I glanced over at the sawbuck table where Sootie's new doll lay. I had taken advantage of the solitude in the cabin to stay up late the previous night working on a new rag doll for her, and it was very nearly finished.

As I had sewed, I remembered Miss Hepplewhite's counsel on the Importance of Thinking and Sewing.

"Thinking and Sewing is very useful when one is upset," she always said.

And to be sure, I was upset. Upset with the intolerable situation in which I found myself. The cabin, now empty with Mr. Russell and Mr. Swan gone to the rendezvous, seemed to close in on me. All I could think of was getting away from this place. My inheritance was in San Francisco, but thanks to Mr. Swan, I had no funds to pay for passage there. It was a vexing situation.

But I couldn't bear the thought of spending a long cold winter here on the bay, surrounded by strangers and people whom I had not known long enough to trust. In the months I'd been here, everyone had disappointed or betrayed me. Everyone except Sootie, that is. I sewed every bit of frustration into the little doll's flour sack body, remembering how Papa had patiently taught me to sew.

"Neat stitches never leave a scar, even in dolls," he told me once with a wink, when he doctored my doll's torn arm.

My stitches were straight and neat. For stuffing, I had used cut-up pieces of a petticoat that was far beyond repair, and for hair, I used strips of cedar bark twisted in the Chinook style.

I looked at the doll with a sense of satisfaction. It was charming. I was certain Sootie would love it. She had been coming by all day long yesterday, begging to see it. But I told her that she had to wait until it was completed. Now it was nearly finished except for some final touches.

Burton was mooing steadily, constantly, like an annoying, buzzing fly. I had milked the beast the evening before and she had kicked out at me, so I was not looking forward to the dangerous chore again. When it became plain that she would not cease her mooing until she was milked, I relented and got out of bed. Her mooing grew louder as I dressed. It grew thunderous as I braided my hair. I had just finished tying on my apron and was heading out the door when the mooing abruptly stopped. I rounded the corner of the cabin and was met by the most curious sight.

Sitting on the stool, milking the cow by the light of a candle, was the figure of a man, singing companionably to himself. His voice rose like a lullaby on the soft morning breeze.

> *Was never a prettier girl than Lucinda,*
> *Dancing across the room that day.*
> *I took one look at that pretty Lucinda,*
> *And grasped her hand and stole her away.*

"Pardon me," I said.

The man looked up and smiled in a disarming way. He was older, Mr. Russell's age perhaps, and he wore a black pressed suit and hat, as if he had just stepped off a steamer ship. His gray beard was neatly trimmed, and when he smiled I detected not one trace of tobacco on his teeth.

He stood up smoothly, tipping his hat politely.

"How do ya do, ma'am. Abraham Black. At your service." His voice was low and throaty.

I was so taken aback that I nearly forgot my manners.

"I'm very pleased to meet you, Mr. Black," I said quickly, curtseying slightly. "I'm Miss Jane Peck. Thank you for milking the cow."

"My pleasure, ma'am," he said. "Lovely young lady like yourself shouldn't have to worry about such things."

My thoughts exactly. I felt a tingle of pleasure at his observation. He was a real gentleman, not some filthy prospecting pioneer. "Did you only just arrive?"

He jerked his head toward the trail that led to the beach. "Schooner came in a little bit ago. From San Francisco."

"Of course," I said. I looked over his shoulder at the pale horse tied to the tree. "You brought a horse?"

He laughed, a low laugh that rumbled in the early morning air. "Oh, Sally and I go everywhere."

"Where are you from?"

"All over, I guess. I don't like to stay in one place too long." He winked. "Don't want to grow moss."

I smiled. "There's no shortage of moss here, I'm afraid. It rains quite a bit."

"I heard there are real good opportunities up this way for a man."

"Why yes, I suppose so. There is the oystering, and the timber."

He nodded thoughtfully, his eyes skimming the length of a long tree. "This used to be a fur-trapping area, if I recall correctly?"

"So I understand. The Hudson's Bay Company had a fur-trapping operation here some years ago."

"Any trappers around anymore?" The question hung in the air.

I shook my head. "I don't believe so."

He seemed to study me. "If you don't mind my saying so, you have lovely hair, Miss Peck. A real unusual shade of red. Reminds me of a lady I knew a long time ago. She had hair the same color as yours and was pretty as a peach, just like you."

I blushed. I was so unused to receiving compliments of any kind. Everything about this gentleman—his clean blacked boots, his brushed coat, his neat hat—spoke to me of civilization.

Just then red-bearded Red Charley appeared from nowhere, cradling an armful of stiff-looking, filthy clothes. I could smell them from where I stood.

"Gal!" he barked, ignoring Mr. Black completely.

I was about to tell him that I had no intention of laundering his clothes when Mr. Black stepped smoothly between us, one hand caressing the gun in his holster.

"I don't believe that's the proper way to address a young lady," Mr. Black said in a dangerously low voice.

Charley looked at Mr. Black as if noticing him for the first time and blustered, "Mind your business, mister."

"I believe you owe Miss Peck an apology," Mr. Black said firmly, his eyes hard. Charley looked like he wanted to let fly at Mr. Black, but after realizing that the other man was a good head taller than him, and armed, he swallowed hard and said, "Course. I 'pologize, Miss Peck." And with that he stomped away quickly.

"Thank you," I said quietly when we were alone again. "I'm afraid that some of the men have been far too long away from civilization."

"Ladies," he said, "should always be treated with respect."

"Would you like to come for supper this evening?" I asked impulsively.

"Really, ma'am, I'm only passing through. I plan to be gone by tomorrow. And I wouldn't want to put you to any trouble."

"It wouldn't be any trouble, Mr. Black. Honestly. I usually cook for a whole gang of men, but they are all away on business at the moment."

"No, really—"

"Please," I begged. "It would be such a delight."

He nodded a little reluctantly. "Thank you kindly. I'd be mighty pleased to have supper with you, Miss Peck."

Mr. Black was nowhere to be seen all day, but just as the sun was beginning to kiss the horizon, he appeared at the cabin door.

Brandywine immediately started to growl low in his throat. With his plump little belly, he was hardly the picture of a fierce hound.

"Brandywine! Stop that this instant," I whispered urgently, embarrassed at the hound's display. After a moment the dog went over to a corner to stare at us with glowering eyes, his belly pouched under him like a plump cushion.

Mr. Black eyed Brandywine coolly.

"Dogs don't seem to like me much these days, Miss Peck. They don't take to traveling men."

I laughed lightly. "Brandywine barks at everything."

Mr. Black removed his hat and smiled at me. I couldn't remember the last time a man had removed his hat for me!

"Animals have their reasons, Miss Peck," he said in an unconcerned voice, and pulled out my chair with a flourish.

It was wonderful to simply sit and talk to him. He brought a great deal of news from the States and was very interested in my opinions. The deep timbre of his voice, his smiling dark eyes, his very words, seemed to weave a spell in the cabin so that I almost believed I was back in Philadelphia and eating supper with one of Papa's friends in the dining room on Walnut Street. Papa had been fond of bringing acquaintances home to supper, and we'd had all manner of people dine at our table—judges, physicians, lawyers, even politicians.

"I own a mine back in California. Gold," Mr. Black said when I inquired as to his occupation.

"Gold. How exciting."

He fished in his pocket and pulled out a watch. It was a thick gold pocket watch with an intricately worked design of a rose on the casing. It glowed softly in the palm of his hand. "This came from my mine."

"It's lovely."

"And it keeps good time, too."

He leaned back in his chair.

"What brings you to Shoalwater Bay?" I asked curiously.

"I have some unfinished business up this way." He stared into the fire. "Loose ends to tie up, you might say."

It seemed rather rude to pry, so I stood up to begin clearing plates. He was on his feet in a flash, helping me.

"Please, I insist," I said. "It's been such a pleasure to have a gentleman in this cabin." I took the plates from him. His food, I noticed, had barely been touched.

"You don't usually have gentlemen, then?" Mr. Black asked, a touch of humor in his voice.

"Mr. Black, I think I can say with some assurance that you are the first *gentleman* to set foot in this cabin. No, let me clarify. The first one to set foot on the bay."

He chuckled.

"No, really," I said. "There is no end to filthy louts in this part of the country. Why, not last week I was propositioned by a man so that he could obtain land!"

"No!"

"Yes, and I had thought that Jehu was a man of honest intentions, for all that he is a sailor."

Mr. Black rubbed his beard thoughtfully. "Sailors are nothing but trouble."

"I couldn't agree more! And then Mr. Swan just up and abandoned me here in this cabin." I leaned forward confidingly. "Not that I'm very surprised—he abandoned his own wife and children in Boston."

"Abandoned his wife, you say?"

"It's shocking, really." I plunged on, happy to have a receptive audience. "But the worst of them all is Mr. Russell!"

"Mr. Russell?" A whisper.

"He is the owner of this cabin, and all he does is order me about as if I were a maid," I said. "And he doesn't make housekeeping at all easy. Why, I'm forever dodging his tobacco."

Mr. Black's eyes shone in the fire glow as he looked about the cabin. "Where is this Russell now?"

91

I shrugged. "Far from here, thank heavens. He and Mr. Swan have gone to the rendezvous."

"Rendezvous?"

"Yes. Governor Stevens has called a meeting of all the Indian tribes in this part of the territory. Mr. Swan and Mr. Russell went along to help translate."

"I see."

I poured coffee and sliced pieces of apple pie I had made especially for the occasion.

"Whereabouts is this rendezvous?" he asked casually.

"Some distance, I believe. I imagine that one of the Chinook would know."

Mr. Black nodded to himself and then looked at me thoughtfully. "So tell me, Miss Peck, what is a fine lady like yourself doing out here in the wilderness?"

I told him the whole story of my sea journey, William Baldt, and the more recent news of Papa's death that had left me stranded here.

Mr. Black's eyes narrowed and he stared into the fire. When he looked back, he had an intense expression in his eyes. "It's always the people closest to you who betray you." Then he seemed to shake himself and stood up. "I believe I'll turn in now. I pitched my tent down past the stream."

I hesitated. "There are mountain cougars in the area."

Mr. Black laughed grimly. "I can manage a few wild beasts, Miss Peck. It's the two-legged variety you have to watch out for."

Then he tipped his hat gallantly and disappeared into the dark night.

I closed the door and went back into the cabin. Mr. Black's piece of pie lay untouched.

Brandywine gave a low whine from the corner.

"Maybe he doesn't care for pie, Brandywine," I said. I looked at his plate from supper. "Or biscuits and gravy."

I set the plate of pie on the floor and the dog bounded over, belly swinging, and began to eat enthusiastically.

"At least someone appreciates my cooking," I said with a sigh.

I woke before dawn, eager to make a nice, hearty breakfast for Mr. Black. I grabbed the coffeepot and headed to the stream that ran alongside the encampment.

It was chilly and still quite dark out, with light just glimmering in the sky. Thick fog hung in the air, and here and there stray shafts of light broke through. Burton was mooing loudly to be milked. She could wait, I decided, until I had the coffee boiling. I stepped carefully in the direction of the stream—the fog so thick it swirled and eddied all around me—and then froze at the sight that met my eyes.

Mr. Black was standing at the stream with his trousers on, suspenders hanging down, his back bare.

He was holding a small mirror and razor and carefully shaving his cheeks. I gasped.

The pale skin of his back was crisscrossed with thick, angry scars, as if someone had taken a whip to him. Or worse.

Mr. Black whirled around, eyes searching, but I stepped quickly behind a tree, my heart beating fast. After a moment, he returned to his shaving, and I carefully made my way back to the cabin, my mind whirling. What had happened to the poor, kind man?

I was still trembling a bit when I heard a soft knock at the door. It was Mr. Black, holding a pail of milk.

"Oh really," I said, pasting on a bright smile. "You shouldn't have."

He smiled. "Now Miss Peck, course I should."

"Would you like some breakfast?"

He shook his head, looking up at the brightening sky. "'Fraid not, ma'am. I think there's a storm brewing, so I best get ahead of it."

"You're leaving already?"

He nodded.

"Wait," I said, and rushed back into the cabin. I took an empty flour sack and wrapped the biscuits from the evening before, and the rest of the pie, and put them both into the sack. "Traveling's hungry work."

"Thank you so much, Miss Peck."

"It was my pleasure," I said.

He pressed something cold into my hand. I looked down to see the gold watch.

"Seems to me, even with the loss of your father, Philadelphia's still your home. This'll pay for you to get to San Francisco. The schooner that brought me will be heading back there tomorrow," he said seriously. "You can catch another ship when you get there."

"Mr. Black, I can't take this—"

He closed my fingers shut over the watch. "You just think about it," he said in a gentle voice.

And then he climbed on his waiting horse and disappeared into the dawn.

Later that morning as I was putting the finishing touches on Sootie's new doll—a handkerchief dress—the little girl came bursting into Mr. Russell's cabin.

"Look, Boston Jane!" she shrieked happily.

She was holding an exquisite china doll. It had a creamy face, pink cheeks, and glossy black hair that matched Sootie's own thick locks. The doll was wearing a pink satin dress with bows and a little ermine stole.

"Sootie," I asked carefully. "Where did you get that doll?"

"Mrs. Frink!"

At that moment Mrs. Frink walked into the cabin. "Hello, Miss Peck," she said cheerily.

Something in me went still.

"How do you like Sootie's new doll? The poor dear was quite beside herself with that dog eating her old one, and why, I just *had* to do something," Mrs. Frink declared breezily.

Sootie clutched the china baby rapturously.

I looked at the rag doll in my hands, at the floursack face and button nose, the bark hair and handkerchief dress. It was so sad-looking compared to the exquisite china doll. A flush of embarrassment rushed through me.

"What do you have there?" Mrs. Frink asked curiously.

I turned away from her, bunching the doll in my apron, a sense of desolation stealing over me. There was no place for me here. This wasn't my home; it never had been.

"Nothing," I whispered dully. "Nothing at all."

By the end of the day, I had booked passage on the schooner to San Francisco.

CHAPTER NINE
or,
A Startling Announcement

For all the time I had spent on the bay, I had precious little to pack.

In short order, all that was left to do was bid my good-byes. I had no idea when Mr. Swan and Mr. Russell would be back, and I wondered if they would even notice I was gone, now that they had Mrs. Frink to cook them chicken suppers and bake crumble cake.

The evening before my departure, I lay awake a long time, watching the flickering fire, with the quiet punctuated by the sounds of Brandywine's restless sleep. He twitched and squirmed, emitting little gruff barks from his throat every now and then, lost in some doggy dream. From a distance came the occasional shouts of voices rising and falling as men finished card games. I tried to comfort myself with the idea that in a few months' time I would be sleeping in a soft bed instead of on a hard, flea-infested bunk, and bathing in a proper tub instead of in a cold stream. There would be clean dresses, and linen sheets, and sweet soap.

And Sally Biddle.

I winced just imagining how she would view my disgraceful situation.

"Just as I predicted," she would say smugly. "I knew Dr. Baldt would come to his senses the moment you stepped off the boat. After all, who would want to marry a girl like you?"

But at least in Philadelphia there were people who could help me. I would visit Papa's solicitor, and he would arrange things. And Mrs. Parker would give me good advice. Why, I could even go back to my old school, the Young Ladies Academy, and assist my teacher, Miss Hepplewhite. After all, I had always received high marks. She would also be invaluable in introducing me into society. The situation was not so dire, I told myself.

Brandywine pressed his nose against my foot, burrowing closer for warmth. It would be winter soon, but I would not see it. I would never see another season on Shoalwater Bay. Never watch the sun melt into the water like sugar dissolving into tea. Never again feel the air grow soft, everything so still that you could practically hear your heart beat.

I shook myself and rolled over, dislodging Brandywine. The beast whined and settled himself against me more firmly. I should be happy to go home, I told myself. I would never have to wash another filthy shirt, cook another unappreciated meal, or milk another ill-tempered cow. I would never have to be disappointed by men who drank too much and gambled away a fortune.

I would be a world away from them all.

The sound of a fiddle hummed insistently in my head.

I was spinning beneath a starry sky, the music rising around me like a whirlwind, the flames of a bonfire licking high into the night. All around me pioneer men swung women about in time to the music. Warm hands clasped my waist, and I looked, and there was Jehu, smiling down at me. Relief surged through me at the familiar sight of his scar, shining bright as a talisman. I felt relief, and something else, something that made my stomach twist in giddy anticipation, and made me lightheaded.

"I'm so happy you're staying, Jane!" he shouted, his voice mingling with the music like a note all its own.

I'm not! I wanted to say, but my throat was so tight that I couldn't make the words come out, and then it didn't seem to matter what I said, because he was leaning down, his lips hovering over mine, and more than anything I wanted one last kiss. The fiddle grew louder and louder, filling my ears, screeching high until suddenly the world tilted crazily, and I blinked and found myself back on Walnut Street.

For a moment all I could do was drink it in—the shouting newsboys, the maids gossiping on their way to their errands, the dogs begging at the butcher shop, the carriages clip-clopping down the cobblestone streets. There was the aroma of baking bread, and fish, manure, and a dozen other smells that mixed and swirled in a way that was only Philadelphia.

I walked quickly down the street to our house, my heart beating rapidly. Walking toward me carrying a basket was a figure I would recognize anywhere. I ran straight into her arms.

"Mrs. Parker!" I cried, hugging my old housekeeper tight. "I've missed you so!"

"Oh, Miss," Mrs. Parker said, her plump face clouding over.

"You must make one of your cherry pies now that I am back," I insisted, tugging her along with me as we walked toward home.

"But Miss Jane," she protested.

And then we were standing in front of our house.

But our house was gone.

Where our parlor had once been situated, a groom led a horse from a stable.

"Miss Jane, I tried to tell you," Mrs. Parker said sadly, her face flushed with unhappiness.

Behind me I heard a soft laugh, a laugh I knew all too well.

Sally Biddle.

I turned around. She was shaking her head at me, blond corkscrew curls bobbing. "Why, if it isn't Jane Peck," Sally Biddle drawled.

My face drained of blood.

Sally pointed her fan at me. "Your house always did bear a great resemblance to a stable."

Somehow I found my voice. "You—you—"

"It was a very good bargain, really," Sally informed me in a silky voice. "When your father died, my papa bought it for a song. I was the one who suggested it, actually."

This wasn't happening.

"Oh, and Jane—I forgot to mention. I'm having a party on Friday. Perhaps you can come." She paused, and laughed softly. "And work in our kitchen!" And then she burst into laughter.

Her laughter stung my ears like breaking glass, and I couldn't bear it. I just picked up my skirts and ran into the street. I ran down the cobblestones, my face wet with tears.

Mrs. Parker's voice rang in my ears.

Watch out, Miss!

The carriage was coming straight at me, swerving wildly.

I screamed once—and then woke up.

The schooner was due to depart in the afternoon, so I set off first thing in the morning to say my farewells. I headed first to Father Joseph's chapel.

It was cool, but the sky was bright and blue. As I followed the path that led to the chapel, I rehearsed what I was going to say to Father Joseph. The gentle priest had fuzzy eyebrows that danced beneath the dome of his bald head when he was excited. That was exactly what they were doing when I arrived at his chapel. He was describing various saints to Kape, who seemed to be on the verge of nodding off.

Kape, the young man who had proposed that I bake pies in exchange for work on the oyster beds, was thus far Father

Joseph's only recruit. Father Joseph was very enthusiastic about converting him to Catholicism. He had baptized him François, but everyone still called him Kape.

"Hello, Father," I said.

"Mademoiselle Jane," Father Joseph said happily. "I was just discussing the saints with young François here."

Kape looked relieved at the interruption.

"Boston Jane," Kape said, patting the shirt he was wearing. It was the one I had sewn for him. "This shirt is very good."

"Would you care to join us?" Father Joseph asked eagerly.

I hesitated for a moment. Father Joseph had been one of my companions on the voyage from Philadelphia, and while the priest had vexed me at first, I had grown fond of him.

"I'm leaving," I said.

Father Joseph raised one fuzzy eyebrow. "Leaving?"

"Yes, I've decided to return to Philadelphia. On today's schooner," I said quickly.

"*Mais pourquoi, Mademoiselle?*" he asked, opening his hands wide, palms up. "This is your home."

The way he said home, with such contentment and certainty, made my unease grow until it was like a heavy ball of unbaked dough in the pit of my stomach.

"Philadelphia is my home," I said quickly. "Truly, I don't belong here. And besides, the oystering venture with Mr. Swan has been a disaster."

"But Mademoiselle, you must give Mr. Swan a second chance. It is Christian to forgive."

I barreled on as if he hadn't even spoken. "I don't fancy spending the rest of my days taking in men's mending."

"Who will make pie?" Kape asked.

"I'm sure Mrs. Frink is quite capable of baking a pie."

Kape seemed unconvinced.

"Have you told Jehu about your plans?" Father Joseph asked quietly.

"I don't believe Jehu's opinion has any bearing on my life," I said stiffly.

"You must at least tell Keer-ukso that you're leaving!"

"I suppose I should," I admitted reluctantly. I had hoped to make a quick escape. "He's at M'Carty's helping mend the roof." With Jehu, I thought.

Father Joseph looked relieved. "Wait a moment." He dug around in a basket in the corner and pulled out two bottles of wine. "Would you mind taking this to M'Carty? For the pain."

"Where did you get them?"

He looked a little shamefaced. "It's communion wine."

Poor Father Joseph was normally firm about Church doctrine, and I imagined that the bishop would not approve of doling out communion wine to men who broke their legs. I took the bottles.

"You shall be missed, Mademoiselle," Father Joseph said, and then he gave me a great hug.

I hugged him back hard, the scratchy wool of his robe grating on my cheeks and soaking up my tears before he could notice them.

The day grew unseasonably warm and humid. By the time I reached M'Carty's homestead, I was damp and uncomfortable. I took off my cape and carried it.

Jehu was perched on the roof, shirtless, his muscled back coated with a fine sheen of sweat.

"Boston Jane!" Keer-ukso called, walking toward me, carrying planks. He wasn't wearing a shirt either! Was I destined to see the bare chest of every man on Shoalwater Bay?

Jehu heard Keer-ukso's shout and peered at me. He scaled down to the ground.

"Something wrong back at the cabin?" he asked, wiping the hair from his forehead.

"Uh, no," I stammered. "Everything's fine."

"What have you got there?"

I held the bottles of wine aloft. "I brought them for M'Carty. From Father Joseph."

"That the only reason you came?" he asked quietly.

Before I could answer, Keer-ukso was at my side. He nodded at the roof, explaining, "We fix roof in Chinook way."

The Chinook way was to use cedar planks, as I knew from helping Keer-ukso myself once. "It looks very good," I assured him, as he and Jehu both retrieved their shirts to put on.

"Come meet Cocumb," Keer-ukso said, taking me by the elbow and leading me into the log cabin.

The last time I had seen M'Carty he had looked strong and fit, even a little full at the belly. Now he was thin and drawn. His leg was propped up on a pile of pillows and secured by two thick sticks bound with a bandage. A Chinook woman with a dark fall of hair was bending over him, her face turned away.

"Is that Miss Peck I see?" M'Carty joked, his smile strained.

The woman gave a firm tug on the bandage around his leg.

"Cocumb!" he barked in pain, struggling to sit up.

But his wife pushed him back to the pillows. M'Carty reached for a whiskey bottle on the side table, but Cocumb beat him to it, swatting his hand away. M'Carty groaned dramatically. Cocumb shook her head, as if scolding a belligerent schoolboy, and turned to us with a sigh.

"Boston Jane," Keer-ukso said, introducing me.

"I'm very pleased to finally meet you," I said, extending my hand.

Cocumb shook it firmly. "I have heard much about you." Like many of the Chinook, she spoke very good English.

I pressed the wine into her hand. "From Father Joseph."

"Good man," M'Carty called from the bed. "I'm nearly plumb out of whiskey."

Cocumb sniffed in disapproval and then turned to me. "Come and have some tea," she offered.

"Thank you very much. That would be lovely."

Cocumb set out tea and freshly made biscuits. I eyed M'Carty's miserable form on the bed. "How did M'Carty break his leg?"

M'Carty groaned dramatically.

Cocumb rolled her eyes. "My husband wanted to fix roof himself."

"I could do it, too!" he complained from the bed.

She and I exchanged a meaningful glance and laughed.

"I wanted you to meet my daughter," Cocumb said. "But I sent her to stay at my father's lodge because my husband is so much work," she finished, with a rueful glance at M'Carty.

"What brings you out here, Miss Peck?" M'Carty asked. "Looking to hire another schooner? 'Cause I don't recommend waiting much longer if you've got oysters to send to San Francisco. I've got a feeling that winter's gonna come early this year. Now, it's just a feeling, mind you, but I'm usually right about these sorts of things."

Jehu's figure suddenly filled the doorway, and I remembered why I had come.

"Actually," I said, marshaling my voice. "Actually, I won't be requiring a schooner." I swallowed hard. "I came to say good-bye."

"Good-bye?" Keer-ukso repeated.

"Yes," I said quickly, before my courage disappeared. "There's a schooner leaving this afternoon bound for San Francisco. I'm going home."

"But how can you pay the fare?" Jehu asked bluntly.

He was so irritating. "My financial affairs are none of your concern."

"Everyone knows Swan gambled away your money."

"This is how I'm paying for my fare," I said in frustration, thrusting out the watch.

Jehu snatched it out of my hand, inspecting it closely. "Who gave this to you?"

"A gentleman gave it to me."

He took a step forward, his eyes turning dark, like the sky over the bay before a storm. "There aren't any gentlemen out here."

"You are most certainly correct on that count, Mr. Scudder," I said, glaring right back at him. "But I assure you, Mr. Abraham Black was a gentleman in all respects."

"Abraham Black?" M'Carty croaked hoarsely from his bed.

"Oh, then you are acquainted with Mr. Black?" I asked eagerly. "Isn't he perfectly charming? It was so refreshing—"

"Where is he now?" M'Carty demanded, pulling himself up and hobbling over using a thick cane, pain etched on his face from the effort.

"Why, I have no idea. He left yesterday."

"Did he say where he was from?" he asked anxiously.

"California, I believe."

"What did he look like?"

"Well, he was about your height, with trim gray hair. He wore a neat black suit."

"Jane," M'Carty asked urgently, "did you tell him where Russell went?"

I didn't understand why M'Carty was so upset. "I told him that Mr. Russell and Mr. Swan had gone to the rendezvous with Governor Stevens."

"Oh Lordy."

"What?"

M'Carty slumped against the wall, his face white. "He's going to kill Russell," he whispered.

CHAPTER TEN

or,
M'Carty's Strange Story

After his startling announcement, M'Carty promptly collapsed on the cabin floor with a groan.

Cocumb shook her head at him. "Bed," she said firmly. She waved an imperious hand, and Keer-ukso and Jehu hauled M'Carty up and carried him to the bed between them.

"What do you mean, he's going to kill Mr. Russell?" I asked, joining the crowd over at the bed.

"Help me sit up, woman," M'Carty groaned to Cocumb, his face strained with pain.

"You are more stubborn than a dog stuck in mud," she said, propping pillows behind him.

M'Carty breathed hard from the exertion of sitting up.

"Mr. Black didn't even know who Mr. Russell was," I said.

M'Carty eyed me sharply. "Oh, he knows Russell, all right. Believe you me. He knows Russell."

"But how?"

"'Cause he was one of 'em."

"One what?"

"A Silencer."

The cabin was quiet for a moment. Finally Keer-ukso asked the question all of us were thinking. "What is a Silencer?"

"It's a mountain man, of course. A trapper. One of the most famous ones."

I had never given any consideration to what Mr. Russell had done prior to coming to Shoalwater Bay. Fur trapper. He surely dressed the part, with his buckskins and rifle.

"Russell worked for the Rocky Mountain Fur Company years ago. Trapped for them. Beaver. Otter. You name it. If it had a hide, he killed it."

It was easy to picture Mr. Russell trekking through the snowy, windswept mountains, carefully tracking animals. Living a life of solitude, with only his horse for company.

As if he knew what I was thinking, M'Carty said, "Russell worked with four other men."

"I thought all mountain men trapped alone."

"That's just talk. Ain't too many men fool enough to live in the wilderness by themselves. If an animal don't get you or a storm don't kill you, your own mind'll turn on you for lack of someone to talk to."

"What about the others?" Jehu asked.

"Well, the other men Russell trapped with were Elijah Barnett, Toby Winston, Jack Meares, and a fellow named Abe Black."

"My Mr. Black?" I asked.

"*Your* Mr. Black?" Jehu demanded.

"I hardly think that you are in a position to say anything. At least Mr. Black's a gentleman. At least he wasn't trying to trick me into—"

M'Carty held up a hand for silence.

Jehu and I stared at each other furiously.

M'Carty shook his head. "Yes, Jane, I believe the man you met was the same man who trapped with Russell." He swallowed hard. "Anyhow, the five of them trapped along the Snake River and into the mountains. They called themselves the Silencers on account of the fact that they didn't leave so much as a rustle of an animal behind them."

Keer-ukso cracked a smile.

"How long did they work together?" I asked.

"I reckon they trapped for near about four years before the accident. This was well over twenty years ago now. They were all young men back then, every one."

"The accident?"

M'Carty's face turned grim. "As Russell tells it, they were trapping along a river, high in the mountains. Now, rivers are where most trappers work 'cause that's where beavers are found. The critters build their homes right in the water. You jest set your trap, put some scent on it, and if you wait long enough the animal will come on out and walk himself right into your trap."

Jehu whistled admiringly.

"Sounds easy, but it was a hard way to make a living. Especially if you were a company man. All your equipment was rented from the company, and so that came out of your pay. You had to work real hard, too, to turn a profit and make it pay off." M'Carty took a breath. "And then of course there's the grizzlies."

"Grizzlies?"

"See, beavers like to live near the rivers. But so do the grizzly bears. They do their fishing there. Many a trapper's been killed by a grizzly while trying to catch a beaver. On the day Abe Black died, they were along a river."

"Died?" I whispered. "But he's not dead! I ate supper with him, I tell you—"

M'Carty held up a finger for quiet. "And I tell you that Abe Black died that day in the mountains."

I shook my head.

M'Carty's voice was pitched low as he described the terrible day. "It was early spring, but there was still snow on the ground. The men had finished for the day and were setting up camp. Except for Abe Black. He said he was going to check one last time on the beaver traps he'd set earlier that day. He didn't want no beaver getting trapped and then some other varmint coming along and eating it before he got to it. So there he was checking on his trap when all of a sudden a grizzly bear came behind him and slashed him across the back."

I gasped, remembering Mr. Black's scarred back.

"The grizzly musta smelled him, 'cause he came up from downriver. Abe grabbed that grizzly, and that grizzly grabbed him back, and its claws just slashed and slashed at his back. The men heard him screaming and came running and shot at the

111

beast, and the bear took off." He took a long swallow of whiskey, draining the bottle. "But it was too late."

"Too late?"

"Abe was dead," M'Carty said with a wince, propping himself up on an elbow. "That grizzly had ripped apart his back and he'd lost a lot of blood. They buried him under some leaves, and took his gear and headed off."

"They just left him there?"

"The ground was too frozen for a proper burial, and he was dead," M'Carty said simply. "And they were in the mountains. They were weeks away from the nearest town, even if they had wanted to haul his body out."

"Why'd they take his gear?"

"If they hadn't taken it, the company would've charged them for it." M'Carty breathed heavily, his face gray from the pain. "Russell was real broke up. He and Abe were like brothers. And then of course, he was the one who had to tell Abe's wife the bad news. Russell says she took to her bed and was dead a week later . . . that Lucy died of pure heartbreak . . . that it was even sadder than Abe dying. Saddest thing he ever seen."

"Lucy," I whispered.

Was never a prettier girl than Lucinda.

"Russell didn't have the heart to trap after that. He spent some time leading pioneers across the mountains, and after a while he headed up here to the bay. And then a few years ago, the rumors started."

"What kind of rumors?" Jehu asked.

"Rumors about a ghost."

I shivered.

M'Carty eyed us appraisingly. "Takes time for stories to travel to these parts. They take their time, but they get here eventually. First we heard how Elijah Barnett went to sleep in his tent a breathing man and never woke up. His partner found him the next morning, his throat cut. He'd been murdered."

Murdered. The word hissed through the cabin.

"Whoever did it left a grizzly paw in his hand."

We all looked at M'Carty.

"Elijah's partner swore that they were the only ones within miles, that there weren't even any Indians around. He was sleeping right next to him and never heard a sound. Never even woke up."

Keer-ukso's eyes widened. *"Memelose,"* he whispered.

Memeloses were spirits of the dead.

M'Carty nodded his head. "That's right. Elijah's partner said the same thing. Said it musta been a ghost. And that's when the rumors started about Abe Black's ghost seeking revenge."

"But Mr. Black's no ghost, I assure you—"

"Toby Winston was next," M'Carty continued. "He was mining for gold in California. They found him dead in a tunnel. Same as Elijah. A grizzly paw in his hand. The men who were in the mine with him swore they never saw nobody come in. They swore to high heaven that only a ghost could've got past that many men without being spotted. The only thing that was unusual was that the hound dog that hung around the camp went crazy, barking his fool head off. That dog was never the same, and they had to shoot it to put it out of its misery."

"Animals see *memeloses*," Keer-ukso said in a knowing voice.

Dogs don't seem to like me much these days, Miss Peck. They don't take to traveling men.

"Go on," I said, my voice a little unsteady now. "What happened next?"

M'Carty took a deep breath. "Jack Meares heard about what happened and sent word to Russell. To warn him to be careful."

"The letter I brought Russell. It was from Missouri," Jehu interjected.

M'Carty nodded. "Jack Meares had a farm there."

"Had?" I asked, my throat tight.

"Jack Meares was murdered nearly nine months ago. His hired hand found him one morning with his throat cut."

"Grizzly bear paw?" Keer-ukso asked.

M'Carty's silence spoke volumes.

"This is ridiculous," I said with a nervous laugh. "Men telling tall tales."

M'Carty looked at me hard. "And now Russell's the only one of the Silencers left."

"But Mr. Black was real. He's no ghost. He can't be," I insisted. "He milked the cow for me. He, he came to supper—"

And didn't eat a bite, a small voice in my head said silkily. *What kind of flesh-and-blood man ignores a cooked meal?*

"Who's to say what he is, Miss Peck. He could be a demon or he could be a man. Either way, one thing's sure. Abe Black's a man who was left for dead and he's come back to kill the last of the men who left him. He's come back for vengeance." M'Carty's voice lowered an octave, and he stared at me. "He's a dead man walking and he's come to kill Russell."

The air went terribly still. Everyone stared at me.

"And you told him where to find him," M'Carty finished grimly.

"This is nonsense!" I cried.

M'Carty snorted.

"Mr. Black is no murderer! He gave me this watch to pay my fare!" I said, looking about wildly for an ally. "Cocumb," I pleaded. "You don't believe this nonsense, do you?" She seemed such a sensible woman.

She sighed heavily. "We have known Mr. Russell since he first arrived on the bay, Jane, and he has spoken of Mr. Black and the other men. And now that Mr. Russell's friends are dead . . . ," she said, her thought trailing off.

M'Carty started barking orders to Jehu and Keer-ukso. "You boys gotta go find Russell, and fast. You gotta find him before Abe Black does."

Jehu turned to Keer-ukso. "You know the area."

"This Black have canoe?" Keer-ukso asked me.

"No, he was on horseback."

He nodded decisively, and looked at M'Carty. "We need canoe."

"You bet, boys! And take my gun, too," M'Carty ordered, pointing to a corner of the room. "You're gonna need it. At least, I sure hope you will. Bullets won't stop no ghost."

"You're going now?" I asked.

"Black left yesterday," Jehu said simply. "But Keer-ukso knows these parts better." He turned to Cocumb.

"Cocumb, we'll finish the roof when we get back. It should hold till then," he said. "Can we borrow some packs and provisions?"

Cocumb nodded and started to dig in a trunk in the corner. Keer-ukso and Jehu began to help her. Watching the swirl of activity in the cabin, I said to no one in particular, "Well, I'll be going now. My boat will be leaving soon." I turned and began walking to the door.

A hand lashed out and grabbed my wrist.

I turned to see Jehu.

"Let go," I said, tugging at my hand.

He stared at me hard, his face working with unnamed emotions as he held my arm firmly but gently. The scar on his cheek twitched. I stared at him for a long tense minute, until he finally croaked, "You can't go."

"Why not?" I demanded.

I looked around the room at Cocumb, M'Carty, and Keer-ukso, who all looked away as if embarrassed. Jehu was holding his breath and looking at me with a strange, desperate expression.

"What?" I snapped.

"You can't go," he repeated.

"I certainly can. And shall. Let go of my arm, please."

Something flickered across Jehu's face, and his deep blue eyes lit up. "You have to come with us!"

"Come with you," I echoed, startled. "Have you gone mad?"

116

"It's. Your. Fault," he said in a low voice, releasing my wrist and stabbing his finger at me.

"What's my fault?" I said, retreating a step toward the door.

"You're the reason a murderer's after Russell. You may as well have just gone and shot him yourself." He shook his head firmly, advancing on me. "You gotta stop being selfish."

"I'm not being selfish!" I exclaimed indignantly, my voice rising. "It's, it's not proper for me to go off into the wilderness. It's, it's—dangerous! And there are wild animals and, and—" I sputtered to a stop as I realized they were all shaking their heads at me, even Cocumb. I turned to Keer-ukso wildly. "Please, tell him that I can't go!"

He and Jehu shared a quiet look.

"Mr. Russell is good man," Keer-ukso said finally.

"This is ridiculous. No one needs to go after him. Mr. Black isn't a ghost, or even a murderer, for that matter," I added. "He's a perfectly polite gentleman."

"Polite or not, those men are still dead, Jane," M'Carty said sharply.

"Even if you're right, what possible use could *I* be?" I demanded. "If he's so dangerous—"

Jehu cut me off in exasperation. "Because you know him, Jane. You know what he looks like. We've never even seen him. And besides, he trusts you. You can help lure him out."

"Lure him out?" I drew myself up, smoothed my skirt. "That's your plan? This is utter foolishness. I have a boat to catch." And with that, I turned and opened the door.

Jehu's shoulders slumped. "Fine. Suit yourself."

"I intend to do just that."

Jehu turned and said loudly, "I guess Mr. Russell was right about her after all."

"What do you mean, he was right about me?" I asked, pausing in the doorway.

Jehu ignored me. "We'll head out to the bay and paddle up as far as we can?"

Keer-ukso nodded, avoiding my gaze. "And then we take river."

M'Carty looked at Cocumb, and then back at Jehu. "You know I'd go with you if I could, boys." He looked at them meaningfully. "If I don't hear from you in two weeks, I'll send word to Toke's village."

Jehu nodded and turned to Keer-ukso, who was holding two bulging packs. "We better get moving."

Wasn't he even going to say good-bye to me?

"Be careful," Cocumb said.

Jehu brushed past me. "We will."

CHAPTER ELEVEN
or,
Jane Peck's Amazing Tonic

I went out to the porch with Cocumb and M'Carty and watched as Jehu and Keer-ukso disappeared into the scrubby woods that led to the beach, holding the canoe aloft. Jehu was moving quickly, his strides long, as if he couldn't get away from me fast enough. Keer-ukso glanced back at me, an expression on his face of . . . what? Disappointment? Frustration? But Jehu never turned back to look at me. Not once.

This wasn't what I wanted. I had wanted to return to Philadelphia with an easy heart and start a new life, a life far from this wild stretch of territory. A life where I would be appreciated and needed.

The sky was still a bright stinging blue and the air sweet, but a dark knot had formed in my belly, and it was turning now, twisting its way up to my throat.

I turned to M'Carty and Cocumb and blurted out, "What did Jehu mean? What did Mr. Russell say about me?"

M'Carty glowered at me. "Ask him yourself." Then he limped back into the cabin without a word.

"Cocumb, you understand, don't you? I have to go back to Philadelphia," I said quickly. "It's very important that I catch this boat."

From inside the cabin came the distinct sounds of a crash and a groan.

Cocumb shook her head.

"Should we see if he's okay?" I asked.

After a moment Cocumb said, "He's fine. He doesn't like to use cane. He's stubborn," she said, looking at me.

I took a breath. "Jehu has no right to expect me to put myself in that kind of danger! A real gentleman would never ask such a thing."

"Boston William asked you to come here. You came."

"Yes, well, that was a mistake that I'm trying to set right by going home. Where I belong."

"Boston Jane, you talk about right."

I stared at her helplessly.

"Mr. Russell, he took you in when Boston William did not come."

"Well, yes, I suppose he did," I said. *But it wasn't my fault William didn't show up!* I wanted to shout.

"And this Mr. Black," Cocumb continued relentlessly. "You are sure he is a good man?"

In the distance a bell announced the imminent departure of the schooner.

"That's my boat," I said miserably.

"Cocumb!" M'Carty hollered.

Cocumb squared her shoulders and said, "You must decide."

She turned and opened the door, and the creaking sound it made reminded me of the squeaky door on Mr. Russell's cabin. All of a sudden I remembered how once before I had chosen to follow my own selfish desires.

And left my dear, sweet papa to die alone in Philadelphia.

"Cocumb," I said before I could take it back. "Do you have another pack?"

She turned back and smiled at me, her eyes glinting with humor. "Of course."

I ran all the way to the beach carrying my pack. If Jehu and Keer-ukso were already on the water, I would never catch them. But when I emerged over the dunes, they were sitting next to the canoe, playing a game of cards as if they didn't have a care in the world.

I gasped, trying to catch my breath.

Jehu threw Keer-ukso a lopsided grin. "Guess you owe me."

Keer-ukso nodded approvingly, and slapped a coin into Jehu's palm.

"You made a bet about whether I was going to change my mind?" I demanded indignantly. "You couldn't possibly have known."

Jehu merely pocketed the coin.

"I can't believe you bet against me," I said to Keer-ukso.

He shrugged. "I win last bet."

"Last bet? What did you bet?" But he only winked at me mysteriously.

Keer-ukso had hold of the canoe and was pushing it into the water. Jehu held a hand out to me to help me into the canoe.

"I'm still going back to Philadelphia," I said to Jehu defiantly. "As soon as we get back."

Jehu wisely said nothing.

The canoe we took fit the three of us and our packs easily. I sat in the middle as Keer-ukso perched in the back, expertly navigating our way along the shoreline. Jehu sat in front of me, paddling in long smooth strokes, taking orders from Keer-ukso. He didn't seem to mind having someone else be captain.

The landscape passed in a blur of thick towering trees. I had never been on this part of the bay, and the rocky shoreline was raw and strangely beautiful, like a magician just waiting to reveal his secrets. This wild stretch of land seemed a world away from our tiny settlement. I peered into the trees and saw a thick shaggy shape loping along, as if it were keeping pace with us. A bear? I leaned over the side of the canoe to get a better look, and then it was gone, disappearing into the foliage.

Jehu was wearing the shirt I had sewn for him, and it was damp with sweat from the exertion of paddling.

"How long is this going to take?" I asked, abruptly realizing that the only dress I had was the one on my back.

"Two, maybe three days by canoe," Keer-ukso said. "And then we hike."

"I should have borrowed a Chinook dress from Cocumb," I muttered under my breath.

"Got a spare pair of pants you can have," Jehu said in a laconic voice.

"It'll be a cold day when I borrow a pair of pants from you, Mr. Scudder."

"'Mr. Scudder' is it now?"

I stared straight ahead, ignoring him.

The sun sank slowly, bathing the bay in a warm red glow. A breeze swept up, filling my nostrils with the scent of salt and seaweed, making me think of long-ago walks along the Philadelphia waterfront with Papa, when we watched the sleek ships return from exotic ports. Philadelphia. My schooner was long gone by now, its hold full of oysters, navigating its way along the coast back to San Francisco.

I shifted around, trying to make myself more comfortable. A thick knot of wood rubbed my posterior in a most annoying way, and I kept rearranging my skirts to avoid it, but to no avail. Finally, I looked down in frustration and saw that it wasn't really a knot at all, but rather a huge chunk of dried, prickly grass, perhaps two hands wide. I reached down and tugged at it, but it just stuck. I pulled with all my might and it came free, and I tumbled rearward in the canoe, landing most ignobly on my backside.

"Sit still, Jane," Jehu ordered from the bow. "You're rocking the canoe."

I sighed in relief and settled myself down again.

And immediately felt a cold rush of water soaking through my skirts.

I observed with alarm that the place where the hunk of grass had been was now a large hole—and water was flowing through.

"Oh dear," I said under my breath.

I looked around desperately for anything to stop the leak, and finally yanked the blanket from my pack and stuffed it through, but I pushed too hard and I heard a distinct crack as rotten wood gave way, making the hole quite enormous.

"Jehu," I said in a cautious voice.

"Yeah?"

"There seems to be a hole in the canoe."

"That's okay," he said absently, his eyes scanning the river ahead for obstructions. "We patched it with grass before we left."

"Yes, but you see," I said nervously, "I just removed the grass."

"What?" he shouted, whirling around to stare at me and nearly dropping his paddle.

Keer-ukso looked over and gasped.

"Why'd you do that?" Jehu shouted.

"Because it was most uncomfortable!" I said. "I've been sitting on it for hours."

"Well, you're gonna be a whole lot more uncomfortable unless you start bailing," he said.

"Paddle for shore!" Keer-ukso ordered, expertly changing the direction of the canoe.

The water was rushing in fast, and there was nothing to bail with except my hands, which I used to no effect. The water was so cold my fingers turned blue.

Quite miraculously the men managed to get us to land before the canoe was entirely flooded. Jehu and Keer-ukso hauled it up on shore and collapsed on the sand, breathing hard from their exertions. After a little bit Keer-ukso got up and went over to the canoe, inspecting it. We joined him, observing the damage. A huge section of wood was missing. It was plain to see that the canoe wasn't seaworthy.

"I'm sorry," I said, twisting my hands. "I didn't mean to sink the canoe."

"It's not your fault," Jehu said with a sigh. "M'Carty didn't keep this canoe in good repair to begin with."

"Can't you fix it?" I asked desperately.

"Too much time to fix," Keer-ukso said with a frown. "Faster to walk."

"What do we do now?"

"We have some supper, sleep, and get an early start," Jehu said, picking up the packs, which had somehow managed to stay mostly dry.

I collected driftwood, and shortly we were sitting around a crackling fire. Keer-ukso passed around some dried venison strips and a loaf of roasted *camas*, a Chinook specialty. It was very sweet, and I was rather fond of it. Between the fire and the food, I was feeling a little better.

An owl hooted softly in the night.

"*Memelose*," Keer-ukso said, scanning the tree line.

"That was an owl," I said irritably. The back of my skirt was still rather damp.

"Yes, it is owl. But *memeloses* speak in voices of animals," Keer-ukso explained patiently.

"I don't believe Mr. Black is a ghost," I said firmly. Except for the pesky little detail of him not eating anything. "Or a murderer. Why, he milked Burton for me! Murderers do not milk cows."

"They don't, huh? Met a lot of murderers in your time?" Jehu asked, the fire glow playing softly across his scarred cheek. The stars were shining down on us from the black sky, and for one long moment Jehu's eyes met mine across the fire. And then he looked away.

"I don't need to. I have always been an excellent judge of character, and I could tell Mr. Black was a decent, gallant gentleman."

"You met him once, Jane."

"Three times," I clarified. "But Miss Hepplewhite says that a first impression is all one needs to—"

"You have a lot to learn about so-called gentlemen," he said, shaking his head.

"Oh I do, do I?" I drew myself up. Jehu could be so condescending sometimes. "I was graduated from Miss Hepplewhite's Young Ladies Academy with top marks. I know all I need to know already."

"There's more to knowing things than schooling."

I stared at him furiously. "Well, I know a lot!"

He folded his arms, his eyelashes low. "Well, if you're so smart, how come you're sitting on a crab?"

"What?"

I leaped up. There was nothing there!

Jehu laughed.

Keer-ukso roared in laughter, too.

"You are the most ill-mannered, filthy, blasted—"

Jehu shook his finger at me. "Now, now, Miss Peck. Wouldn't want you to say anything *Miss Hepplewhite* would disapprove of!"

Still chuckling, Jehu and Keer-ukso got up and retrieved bedrolls from their packs. They rolled them out on the sand and began to lie down.

"Where is the tent?" I asked.

"Tent?" Jehu repeated.

"Yes, the tent. Where we sleep," I said slowly, as if I were explaining something to a very small child. "To protect us from wild animals and such."

Keer-ukso said, "No tent."

"You didn't bring a tent?" I asked, aghast.

"Tent is heavy," Keer-ukso explained.

"But we'll be right out in the open!" I said, waving a hand at the darkness edging in from all directions. "Just look!" It was one thing to sleep in Mr. Russell's cabin, but it was quite another to sleep on the beach in plain view. "Anyone or anything could just sneak up on us!"

"Nothing's going to sneak up on us."

"Well, this is most poorly planned," I said. "I am going to go search for shelter."

I trudged up over the dunes and walked for a time. Then, in the distance, I spotted it. Not two hundred yards away was a log cabin.

"Hello!" I called, but no one answered.

I opened the door and peered inside. The cabin had clearly not been lived in for some time and smelled musty with disuse. The roof appeared to be caving in on one end, but it seemed to me it would protect us for one night. There were two rough bunks in its spacious interior.

I reported the good news to the men, who warily returned with me.

"Very old. Probably Hudson's Bay Company man," Keerukso said, inspecting the cabin.

"Seems okay," Jehu acknowledged.

"It will protect us from the elements," I pointed out.

Jehu yawned widely. "Right. Let's move our things and get some sleep."

We moved the provisions and the bedrolls, and kindled a new fire. I took one bunk, and Keer-ukso the other, and Jehu settled down on the dirt floor by the fire and closed his eyes. A moment later, I looked across the shack to see that Keer-ukso was asleep, too.

"You can't both just go to sleep! Someone has to stay awake and keep watch!"

"Great idea. Why don't you go first," Jehu said, and then turned on his side.

I heard something that sounded like a snore coming from Keer-ukso's general direction.

"You're not really asleep, Keer-ukso," I said suspiciously. "Who's going to stay awake and guard the camp?"

"I choose Boston Jane," he said sleepily.

"Seconded," Jehu added with a loud yawn. "Just go to sleep, Jane. We don't need a watch. And we've got a lot of territory to cover in the morning."

There was a scuffling sound from outside the cabin. "Did you hear that? It sounds like someone's right outside."

"Probably just grizzly bear," Keer-ukso said.

"Grizzly bear? But I thought grizzly bears lived by rivers. Do you think one wandered this close to the beach—"

"Jane," Jehu groaned. "He's just trying to rile you up."

Soft chuckling came from Keer-ukso's bunk.

"It's not amusing," I muttered, tugging my cape up to my chin and looking around fearfully. My blanket was still sopping wet from plugging up the hole.

All was quiet for a moment. And then the distinct sound of growling came at me from the blackness behind Jehu. I sat bolt upright.

"Jehu, what was that?"

The growling abruptly turned into soft chuckling, and then full-throated laughs, and soon Keer-ukso was roaring in laughter, too.

"You're both impossible!" I flipped away from them and stared into the blackness, determined to guard the encampment. My vigilance was the only thing standing between us and certain death.

There was no way I was going to fall asleep.

> Was never a prettier girl than Lucinda,
> Strolling down the aisle that day.
> I kissed the lips of my bride Lucinda,
> And grasped her hand and swept her away.

The melancholy voice whispered in my dreams, thin as a ribbon, tugging at me, pulling at my eyelids, dragging me up from a deep sleep. There was so much pain in the song, such an aching sorrow that I had to open my eyes.

I looked up to see a rough-hewn roof and warm firelight flickering on wooden walls. Momentarily disoriented, I then remembered I was in the trapper's cabin. I heard the reassuring sound of Jehu snoring softly.

> Was never a prettier girl than Lucinda.

I turned to the voice.

He was sitting by the fire, across from Jehu's sleeping form, digging a stick in the dying embers. The song was soft, rising like a sad wail on the dark night, dancing high into the stars. His white starched shirt seemed to glow in the cabin, unearthly, and his pale horse nickered softly in the distance.

"Mr. Black," I whispered, but he didn't seem to see me.

He kept stirring the coals, the flames rising now, sending sparks high. Was this sorrowful man a murderer?

An owl hooted softly in the night and Mr. Black turned to me, his dark eyes glowing in the firelight.

"It's always the people closest to you who betray you," he said, his voice like quicksilver.

And then as he stirred the coals, the embers seemed to swirl out of the fire, flying through the air at me. They landed with biting stings on my arms and legs. I slapped them away, but no matter how fast I put the embers out, more of them landed, burning me, stinging. I slapped them away from my arms, my face, and then—

I woke with a start. It was morning, and gray light filtered in the windows.

My face felt hot and itchy. I looked down at my arms, touched my cheeks, and groaned. I was covered with little red, itching bumps.

Fleas. The cabin was positively teeming with them. "Oof," I said scratching. "Blasted pests."

Keer-ukso was sitting up now, and scratching madly at his legs. "Fleas are most troublesome."

Jehu had gotten the worst of it, sleeping on the ground. His face was puffy and red. He scratched furiously at his arms. "Well, now we know why they abandoned the cabin," he said pointedly.

"I didn't know!" I wailed.

"Maybe water help," Keer-ukso suggested, and so we all trooped down to the bay and doused our burning skin with water. It cooled the itching temporarily, but a moment later the searing sensation was back.

"If we'd had a tent in the first place, we wouldn't have had to sleep in that flea-infested cabin," I pointed out.

"The cabin was your idea," Jehu said, irritable now.

"Well, you obviously don't know anything about the wilderness, and I'm counting on you to protect me. We're clearly not prepared for this expedition. We have no tent, and no medical supplies, and only one rifle."

"Not to mention no canoe," Jehu added wryly.

I reddened but continued. "I think we should turn around and go back and get adequate supplies and maybe even some more men. Then I wouldn't need to come at all!"

"We went over this," Jehu said, scratching at his neck. "We can't lose time, and we need you because you're the only one who knows what he looks like. We might as well get moving. It's gonna take us a lot longer by foot."

The morning dragged by slowly as we walked along in silence. The sky was as gray and grizzly as it had been blue the day before. Keer-ukso led us through the winding woods, with only the occasional sound of scratching breaking the quiet. We were all quite miserable. When we paused for a drink of water, I saw that Jehu's face bore raised red welts from where he had scratched himself raw. He scratched a patch of arm in a determined way.

"You shouldn't scratch," I said. "Papa always said that scratching does more harm than good."

"Thanks for the hint," he said shortly.

"There is no need to be unpleasant, Jehu."

He made a disgruntled sort of sound, got up, and started walking again.

I picked up my pack reluctantly and started after them—and that was when I saw a green feathery plant.

What had Mr. Swan said? *Toke told me that this plant is quite therapeutic for all manner of skin ailments. Apparently one is supposed to put the leaf directly on the skin.*

I plucked a small shoot and rubbed it gently on my arm. It immediately felt better.

I hoisted my pack and raced after them with a handful of stems.

"Wait!" I shouted. "I found a cure!"

They paused and regarded me dubiously.

With a flourish, I presented them each with a portion of the leaves. "Just rub them on your skin," I said.

They looked at me warily but did as I instructed.

Jehu looked a little disgusted at the thought, but Keer-ukso put them right on his cheek. He sighed happily. Then Jehu placed his leaves eagerly on his face. For a moment it seemed that they wouldn't work and then his eyes fluttered shut. He gave a moan of relief.

"Now, that's what I call a mighty fine tonic."

I smiled triumphantly. "Remind me to apply for a patent when we're back in civilization. I can call it Miss Jane Peck's Amazing Tonic."

"Cures all ills!" he quipped.

CHAPTER TWELVE
or,
A Powerful Smell

After soothing our skin, we were filled with renewed vigor and seemed to cover a great deal of ground.

"You sure do have your moments, Jane," Jehu said, handing me a sturdy stick. His face still looked terrible, but he was clearly feeling better.

"Mr. Swan mentioned something once."

"It's a good trick. He's a clever man."

"Oh, he's clever all right," I said disdainfully. "He's so clever he gambled away all our money."

Jehu just stared straight ahead.

"Do you know that he never even apologized?" I said, stopping and putting my hands on my waist. "All he can talk about is how wonderful Mrs. Frink is!"

He rubbed the top of his own walking stick. "Maybe he feels ashamed."

"He should feel ashamed," I retorted. "If I never sew a shirt again, it will be too soon."

Jehu looked as if he wanted to say something, but he simply sighed and said, "Come on. It'll be getting dark."

When we finally stopped for the night, I pulled my boots off and massaged my poor feet. They were swollen and throbbed, and there was an angry-looking blister on one of my heels. Clearly my boots had not been designed for any length of walking.

"I wonder what Mrs. Frink would do in a situation like this," I said, eyeing my poor feet sadly.

"She'd probably get out her rifle and shoot us some supper," Jehu said. "And help gather firewood."

I ignored his subtle hint. "Why does everybody like Mrs. Frink so much?" I asked.

Jehu rubbed his scar thoughtfully. "Well, I reckon it's because she's got the charm."

"But I'm charming," I huffed.

Keer-ukso raised a skeptical eyebrow.

"Actually, Jane," Jehu said carefully, "you're kind of, well, prickly."

"What means prickly?" Keer-ukso asked curiously.

Jehu touched the tip of his knife. "Sharp."

"Well, if I am prickly, it's because I've got reason to be!" I burst out. "My betrothed married someone else, my papa died, and now I'm chasing after a filthy man who likes to spit at me!"

"Prickly," Keer-ukso murmured, nodding his head at Jehu in agreement.

We had some more *camas* for supper and set out our bedrolls around the fire.

"Who is going to stay up and watch tonight?" I asked.

Jehu groaned. "You're not starting with that again, are you?"

"We're in the wilderness," I said. "It's dangerous. What if a bear attacks us?"

Jehu closed his eyes and tugged up his blanket, murmuring, "As long as it doesn't wake me up, I don't care." And with that he flipped over.

"Keer-ukso?" I asked.

He yawned widely.

"Please!" I begged. "It's dangerous."

He nodded reluctantly. "You sleep, Boston Jane."

It seemed I had just fallen asleep when I awoke to a rustle in the woods. Keer-ukso was sound asleep, and the fire was mere embers. I could see nothing in the thick blackness. I waited to hear another noise, but when after a moment all was still silent, I fell back into an uneasy sleep. The next morning when I went to organize breakfast, I noticed that one of the packs containing food had been untied.

"Someone's been in the pack," I said.

Jehu wandered over, blinking sleepily. "As long as they didn't take the coffee."

"The dried salmon is gone."

"Probably just some animal," Jehu said, grabbing the coffeepot and heading to the stream, as if someone stealing from the pack was a trifle not be concerned about.

"What kind of animal unties a pack?"

His words echoed to me. "A hungry one."

Jehu was perfectly frustrating, and so when he offered to

take up the lead, staking out a trail, I was happy to remain behind and walk with Keer-ukso. The climb was getting steeper now, and I was having a hard time keeping up; my skirt and thick petticoats kept tripping me. I longed again for my Chinook bark skirt. It was so much easier to walk in.

My shoulders ached. My pack was like a leaden weight. "My pack's too heavy," I complained.

Keer-ukso stopped.

"Truly it is," I said in what I hoped was a persuasive voice.

He shrugged. "I carry."

"Really?"

He gave a small smile.

"Thank you so much," I said effusively.

We stopped and loaded my pack into his. Keer-ukso tested the weight. Then he slung it on his back. "Come."

"Really, Keer-ukso, you are a true gentleman."

He rolled his eyes at me and we walked along in amiable silence.

I was looking straight ahead when my foot hit a thick root I never saw, and I felt myself falling forward.

"*Kloshe nanitch*," Keer-ukso said, grabbing me by the elbow.

"What?"

"I say to be careful," Keer-ukso said, shaking his head. "Boston Jane, you must learn Jargon."

I thought for a moment. "What did you and Jehu say that night in the cabin with William Baldt?"

Keer-ukso grinned. "Jehu, he said, '*Yaka kahkwa pelton.*'"

"What does that mean?"

"'This man, he is a fool.'"

"And what did you say?" I asked.

"I said, 'Certainly,'" he explained, his face mock serious. "'And he resembles a mouse.'"

I laughed. "Maybe I should learn the Jargon after all. Although I'm not very clever when it comes to languages."

"Champ learned Chinook. You say you not smart like Champ?"

Champ was a filthy, drunken, flea-ridden, no account man who had infected the entire village with smallpox.

"Mrs. Frink ask me to teach her Jargon," Keer-ukso said with a twinkle in his eye.

"She did?" Mrs. Frink was learning the Jargon before me?

"But I tell her no, she learn Jargon from Mr. Swan," he said with a knowing smile.

"Teach me some Jargon," I ordered urgently.

Keer-ukso looked pleased. A shiny black crow was perched on a tree, eyeing us carefully as if we were a possible meal. "That is *kawkaw*," he said.

"You mean the sound it makes?"

"*Kawkaw* means that bird."

"Are there are a lot of words like *kawkaw* in the Jargon? Words that are named after what they sound like?" This seemed to me a very practical idea. Much easier than conversational French.

"Yes." He paused and put his hand over my chest. My heart

thudded rapidly under his warm touch. *"Tumtum,"* he whispered, his voice tickling my ear.

"Heart?"

He nodded and then burst into laughter. *"Heehee!"* he said.

"Heehee is funny?"

He shook his head. I tried again. "Laughter?"

"Good, Boston Jane. *Hyak cooley!"*

"What's that?"

He started running up the path and disappeared into the dark woods. *"Hyak cooley!"* he called playfully.

I took off after him. I knew what that meant.

Run fast.

It was dusk when we finally caught up with Jehu. He had already set up camp and kindled a fire.

"Took you long enough," Jehu said, stoking the fire. There was a pot of coffee warming.

"Keer-ukso, why don't you sit down and rest, and I'll pour you a cup of coffee. I'm very good at pouring coffee," I said with my most winning smile. In truth, Pouring Tea and Coffee had been part of the curriculum at the Young Ladies Academy.

Keer-ukso grinned and dropped his pack, stretching his muscles.

"Here you go," I said, handing Keer-ukso the cup. "Now let me see, what is there for supper?"

"Well, unless you baked a pie, it looks like we've got more venison and *camas,"* Jehu said.

I gave him a level gaze. "I'm sure Cocumb packed more than *camas*. Let me look in the sack, if you please."

"Be my guest," Jehu said, tossing me his pack.

There were some Indian meal, salt pork, and a small jar of molasses. "Excellent. I'll make fisherman's pudding. After all, Keer-ukso cannot be expected to carry my pack all day on stringy venison and *camas*."

"You carried her pack?" Jehu asked, astonished.

Keer-ukso sipped his coffee.

Fisherman's pudding involved frying up salt pork, then adding Indian meal, some water, and molasses. It was very hearty, and a favorite dish of all on Shoalwater Bay. I had it ready in no time. And I could tell by the way Jehu and Keer-ukso perked up that their mouths were watering.

I served Keer-ukso a large portion first. "Here you are," I said, handing him a heaping tin bowl. He smiled at Jehu and dug in with gusto.

Next I handed Jehu a bowl. He poked around in it with his spoon.

"Hey, there's no pork in mine," he exclaimed indignantly.

"Keer-ukso worked very hard today," I said in a firm voice.

Keer-ukso chewed enthusiastically, smacking his lips.

I served myself a dish and sat down. "What shall we talk about?"

"How about how I didn't get any pork," Jehu said, and got up and went over to the fire. He picked up the pot and began fishing pieces of pork out of it, popping them directly into his mouth.

"Perhaps we can discuss the benefits of proper table manners," I suggested.

"Perhaps we can talk about what we're going to do when we catch up with this murderer," Jehu retorted.

"That is hardly appropriate supper conversation. Keer-ukso, what do you think we should talk about?" I put my hand on Keer-ukso's arm, appealing to him with my eyes.

Keer-ukso looked down at my hand for a long moment and then over at Jehu. "Boston Jane is good Boston woman. Boston Jane make supper and speak Jargon. Make best wife."

Jehu belched loudly.

I beamed at Jehu. "Obviously, *some* of the gentlemen around here appreciate me."

Keer-ukso added slowly, "Maybe I marry her and get land."

I looked at Keer-ukso in shock. He grinned at me mischievously.

Jehu, who had just taken a bite, began choking with laughter, his eyes watering.

"Keer-ukso!" I huffed, and got up and stormed off into the woods. Really, I couldn't believe Keer-ukso. No doubt Jehu's bad behavior was influencing him.

As I departed, I heard their laughter echoing after me.

"Just for that, you can do the dishes!" I shouted.

I awoke to freezing darkness and a rustling sound.

The useless men had fallen asleep, naturally, and allowed the fire to go out. A grizzly bear could attack us in the middle of the night, and neither one of them would even raise an eyelid.

"Who's there?" I called nervously.

Another rustle.

I thought of Mr. Black wandering around in the woods. What if that was him? What if he was tracking us?

"Jehu!" I hissed, but he just grumbled and flipped over, mumbling into his pack.

I shook my head. I carefully took hold of M'Carty's rifle. If Mrs. Frink could shoot a coyote, I could shoot at a man. Or a ghost, I thought shakily.

The rustling grew louder as I approached a thick shrub. My arms were quaking and the rifle was bobbing up and down. As I leaped around the bush, there was a flash of black and white fur, and then a terrible scent exploded over me.

I fell back, and the rifle shot into the sky.

"Boston Jane!" Keer-ukso shouted, crashing through the bushes. He froze when he smelled me. Jehu was right behind him.

"Oh, Jane," Jehu gasped, turning his head away from me. "That is one powerful smell."

"What happened?" I wailed.

"Looks like that skunk got you," Jehu said, watching as a bushy tail disappeared into the brush.

"But I thought it was Mr. Black!" I moaned, overcome by the wretched smell, which seemed to have sunk into my very skin.

Keer-ukso giggled. Giggled!

"This isn't amusing!" I shouted. "This is the only dress I

have with me. What am I to do?" It was unbearable. I could barely stand the smell of myself.

"Perhaps," Jehu suggested, wrinkling his nose, "you might consider spending the rest of the night over there." He eyed a secluded rock group far away from the fire.

I had hoped it had all been a bad dream, but when I woke in the morning I still smelled very disagreeable. Both men made a point of walking well ahead of me. Now in addition to having sore feet, I smelled. I was very cross indeed.

When we stopped for lunch, I dug around in the pack for the jar of molasses, but it was gone.

"Someone stole the molasses!"

"The skunk probably got it," Jehu said, unconcerned. "Deserved it for the fright you gave him."

I glared at him.

"Maybe you leave at camp," Keer-ukso said soothingly.

"I packed it. I know I did."

I thought about it the whole time we hiked, and when we set up camp that evening I asked Keer-ukso what we should do to keep the provisions safe from animals. "We're going to starve at this rate."

"Hang packs in tree," he said.

I clapped. "What a splendid idea."

After supper I piled all the remaining food in one of the packs, grabbed a hank of rope, and went over to a tall tree not far from where we had set up camp. I stood there for a long moment, wondering how to rig the pack.

"You really want to hang that pack, eh?" Jehu said.

"I don't want the animals to eat any more of our provisions," I said firmly.

"Let me have that rope," he said, and I gave him the length of rope. He flung one end over a tall branch and then secured it to the pack. He hoisted the pack up and proceeded to tie the other end to the tree trunk.

"You want to learn something useful?" he asked, gesturing for me to come over to the trunk.

"I suppose so."

"I'm gonna teach you how to tie a good knot," Jehu said.

"A knot?"

"A knot can save your life. Every sailor knows that. Here. Take one end of the rope. Now, this is the rabbit."

"The rabbit?" I asked quizzically.

He grinned. "That's right. Now, all you need to do is make the rabbit," he said, looping the middle of the rope, "run out of the hole, hop around the tree, and back down the hole again." He fed the rope through the loop and pulled tight. The knot held strongly.

"You try," he said.

I took the rope and followed his instructions, but I must have done something wrong, for it fell apart. "This rabbit is not interested in going into its hole," I said.

He laughed. "Try again, Jane."

I did, and to my utter astonishment, the knot held.

"Well done," he said in approval. "Now let's get some sleep."

The men fell asleep, but I stayed awake, listening. After a bit I drifted off, then was abruptly awakened by a noise. I blinked my eyes open. It was still dark, but I heard birds and knew that it was nearly morning.

And then I saw the bear in our tree.

I seized the rifle and crept to the bottom of the tree, staring into the blackness, trying to make out how big it was. It was so bulky and shaggy-looking that it quite possibly was a grizzly. There was a rustle as the bear inched forward onto the branch from which our packs were hanging. From the ground I could smell his tremendous gamy scent. Could he likewise detect the pungent aroma of skunk that emanated from me?

As if to answer my thought, the bear said, "Phew!"

I looked up, cocking the rifle.

"Don't shoot!" the bear shouted.

I was so startled that I screamed.

A grizzled full-bearded man was dangling from the tree, my pack on his arm.

CHAPTER THIRTEEN
or,
Introducing Mr. Hairy

"I knew it!" I shouted triumphantly. "I knew someone was stealing our food."

Keer-ukso and Jehu were staring up at the tree with stunned expressions. They had come running when I screamed, their hair mussed from sleep, and Jehu was carrying a partially burning log from the campfire.

"And it looks like that *someone* is up in the tree," Jehu observed dryly.

"Should I shoot him?"

"Don't shoot!" the voice in the tree begged huskily.

Jehu stepped forward and sighed. "Come on down, or I can't be responsible for her shooting you."

My pack fell to the ground, and a moment later the man followed it with a crash.

"Oooof!" he groaned as he struck the ground.

The man stood up, and the light from Jehu's torch

illuminated the strange bulky figure. He was wearing some sort of capelike covering made up of various animal skins, and a wretched smell emanated from it.

"And you thought *I* smelled bad?" I asked, taking a step back.

"Skunk got ya, eh, gal?" the man cackled.

Keer-ukso's eyes narrowed in recognition. "Hairy Bill," he said in a flat voice.

"Pleased to meet ya, ma'am," Hairy Bill said, bowing low.

"The man who was kicked off of Shoalwater Bay?" I asked.

Keer-ukso nodded. "For stealing."

"I didn't steal nothing. That's a lie," Hairy Bill declared in an indignant voice.

"You took our molasses," I pointed out.

"And salmon," Keer-ukso added.

Hairy Bill bit his lip.

"The molasses, if you please," I said, putting my hand out.

He reached into his cape, a little reluctantly, and then pulled out the jar and handed it to me. It was half empty and the entire jar was sticky and covered with bits of fur and fluff.

"Did you use your fingers?" I demanded, eyeing his filthy hands.

He shrugged. "Ain't got no spoon."

I shook my head in disgust and handed the jar back. "You can keep it."

Hairy Bill snatched it quickly and squirreled it away in

his voluminous cape. "Thank you, ma'am. I heard you were a nice lady."

"Why are you following us? Don't you have a home to go to?"

"My wife kicked me out," he said in a small, sad voice.

I was quite certain she had very good reason, considering the poor character of the man. "Where is she?"

"Richmond, Virginia."

I gave him a long look. Really, we needed to get rid of this man or we would starve to death.

"Mr. Hairy," I said finally, "I do believe if you took the time to clean yourself up, and apologized, she would quite likely take you back."

"You really think she'd take me back?" he asked, hope shining in his eyes.

I certainly wouldn't, but at least it would get him to the other side of the country. "I'm sure she would consider it, especially if you took my advice about the bath."

He scratched his head, and then he beamed at me as if he found the notion appealing. "Why, ma'am, that's a mighty fine idea. I believe I will go home and apologize. In fact, I believe I'll get moving right after I have some victuals." He looked at me beseechingly. "A man can't walk on an empty stomach."

Jehu snorted.

"But you've been stealing our food for days," I said. I was not at all inclined to cook for this man.

"Jane," Jehu said, sounding tired. "Just give him something to eat."

"Yeah, the least ya can do is feed me!" Hairy Bill whined.

Keer-ukso snatched the rifle out of my hands and pointed the gun straight at Hairy Bill. "Eat and then you go."

Hairy Bill held up his hands. "I promise. You have my word."

"Word of thief," Keer-ukso grumbled.

By that time, the sun was creeping up over the horizon, so I cooked breakfast for all of us. As our supplies were somewhat lower because of Hairy Bill's pilfering, I used the Indian meal to make johnny cakes. Hairy Bill inhaled every scrap I placed in front of him.

"That was mighty tasty, ma'am," Hairy Bill said, wiping his mouth with what appeared to be a fox's tail dangling from the cape.

"That is a rather unusual cape you have there," I observed.

"Thankee," he said, looking pleased. "And it's real warm, too."

"Not to mention it probably keeps the other animals away," Jehu added dryly.

Hairy Bill looked affronted. He tugged up his furry cape and said, "I best be going now."

Keer-ukso nodded in agreement, fingering the rifle.

And with that Hairy Bill got up and loped away, looking very much like the bear I had mistaken him for. Something occurred to me.

"Mr. Hairy," I shouted.

He paused, looking back over his furry shoulder.

"How long ago exactly did your wife kick you out?"

"I reckon it's been about, well, fifteen years now, give or take a few."

"Fifteen years," I said. "I see. Well, good luck anyway."

Hairy Bill disappeared into the sunrise.

Jehu shook his head. "He's gonna need it."

There seemed little point in going back to bed, so we packed up and set out in the cool morning light.

"We should have checked his pockets," I said, as we walked along.

There was the distinct sound of a crash behind us.

"Oh dear," I said. "He's still following us, isn't he?"

Keer-ukso weighed the rifle in his hands.

"Not if he's smart," Jehu said.

"Whatever gave you the impression that he was smart?" I asked.

Jehu chuckled.

We tromped along until we reached a creek. It was flooded, and water rushed down angrily.

"No!" Keer-ukso said with an audible groan.

"What's wrong?" I asked.

"Big tree for crossing, it is gone," Keer-ukso said, pointing. A long, thick tree lay in the creek, partially submerged in the deep water.

"That was the only way across?" Jehu asked, scratching his head.

"Fastest way," Keer-ukso said.

I surveyed the creek. Another tree, a slender one, had fallen across, forming a natural bridge. "What about that tree?" I suggested.

Jehu said doubtfully, "I don't think it will hold us. If we could just get across somehow and rig a rope . . ." His voice trailed off.

Keer-ukso was shaking his head. "Mr. Russell," he said hollowly.

Something about the expression on Keer-ukso's face shook me, and I suddenly knew what I had to do. I went over to Jehu's pack and took out the bundle of rope. Using the sailor's knot Jehu had taught me, I tied one end around my waist, and the other end around the trunk of a thick, sturdy tree. Then I walked to the edge of the creek where the slender tree bridge awaited me.

"Jane, what are you doing?" Jehu asked.

"I'm going across. I'm light enough. When I get to the other side, I'll tie the rope on that tree over there and then you can come across using that. After all, you showed me how to tie that knot," I said, trying to put on a brave face.

"You can't be serious. What if you fall?"

I patted the rope around my waist, and swallowed hard. "Then you drag me up."

And with that I took a tentative step onto the bridge.

"Jane—no!" Jehu shouted, moving quickly toward me. "You're scared of heights, and—"

But his voice was fading, and I just looked forward, walking slowly, foot after foot. The next thing I knew I was standing in the middle of the bridge. For a moment I wavered. The wind seemed to whip up, I felt the wood bow beneath my weight, and fear crackled through me like lightning.

"Jane!" Jehu called in a strangled voice.

I stood there, paralyzed. I blinked, and when I opened my eyes, I was standing on a rooftop in Philadelphia, and Jebediah Parker was right there beside me.

"Come on, Jane! It's easy," he called gaily.

He scampered ahead of me along the high rooftop, his feet sure, his arms wide. I blinked again and he was gone, and I was standing over the raging water. But it didn't matter, because I knew I could do it. After all, I had been beset by tragedy after tragedy—William Baldt had abandoned me and my father had died—but I was still here, and I was strong.

Most of all, I remembered that I, Jane Peck, was the best spitter in all of Philadelphia.

I looked down into all that rushing water.

And spit.

When I looked back at Jehu, his face had gone white. But I just winked . . . and walked to the other side.

Jehu's eyes were shining when he finally made it over. "I knew you had it in you," he said, his voice thick with emotion. He gripped my shoulders hard as if he were afraid I would disappear.

My heart was full to bursting. "See, I really was the best spitter in all of Philadelphia!"

152

"Among other things," he said, his body moving closer to mine.

"Like what?" I asked, transfixed by the way one thick dark curl hung over his forehead.

He traced his finger along my nose. "I'll bet you were the prettiest girl in all of Philadelphia."

"Maybe." I gulped.

"And I'm sure you had the best manners."

"Possibly."

His finger touched my chin gently, tilting it up, and I stared straight into his blue eyes, waiting.

"Oh, Jane," he whispered, and then he pulled me into his chest and hugged me hard, his hand smoothing my hair.

I closed my eyes, listening to the steady thumping of his heart, and smiled.

The day grew colder, frosty even, but Jehu's warm smile and firm hand clasping mine kept me toasty straight through.

Soon, though, even Jehu's attentions could not stop my feet from becoming numb with cold. By the time the sun was falling, I was frozen straight through, and tripping from the sheer lack of feeling in my feet. Even Jehu and Keer-ukso were feeling the effects of the cold weather. Jehu's lips were tinged with blue.

Jehu dumped the packs and pushed me gently down in the pile. "Wait here," he said, and he and Keer-ukso disappeared.

I reached into a pack and pulled a blanket around me, a dizzy exhaustion stealing over my body. My eyes fluttered shut. All I wanted was to be back home in Philadelphia, sitting in our warm parlor on Walnut Street. I believe I would have given anything for a bath and a proper bed and a slice of Mrs. Parker's cherry pie.

And then suddenly I could feel the heat of a crackling fire. I opened my eyes, hardly believing, and there was Papa sitting in his chair, smoking his pipe, his cheeks flush with good health. The smoke seemed to linger in the air, hovering on the edge of my senses.

Papa shook my shoulders gently, concern in his eyes. "Are you okay, Janey?"

He was shaking me hard, but when I blinked, there was Jehu.

"Are you okay, Jane?" he asked urgently.

I swallowed hard, looking around for Papa in confusion. It was now dark, and I was sitting on the cold ground, a blanket and some packs around me. I looked up at him and nodded mutely.

"Let's go, then," he said, helping me up. "We found a good place to camp for the night."

The "good place" they found was a dank, dirty cave. It smelled awful, as if some animal had lived in it, which was probably the truth. The ceiling was so low I couldn't stand properly, and roots dangled and poked into my hair. It was perfectly dreadful.

"This is actually worse than Mr. Russell's cabin," I said despondently, crouching down on the ground. "I never thought I'd see the day that I'd long for that place."

"Keer-ukso thinks there's a storm brewing, and so do I, and we don't want to get caught without shelter," Jehu said firmly.

"What if this is a grizzly bear's cave?" I asked. "What if the bear is out hunting, and comes back and finds us here?"

Keer-ukso shook his head firmly. "Not bear cave. Too small."

"Oh good, that's a relief," I said, slumping against the cold wall.

"Wolf cave," he clarified, holding up what appeared to be the bones of a small animal, no doubt the wolf's most recent supper.

I threw my hands up. "Oh lovely. Wolf," I said sarcastically.

"Let us handle things," Jehu said soothingly.

And handle things they did. Jehu kindled a fire, which promptly went out when the wind whipped through the cave. He kindled it again and the wind snuffed it again. After the fire went out a third time, I suggested that they hang one of the blankets across the entrance, leaving a small hole for the smoke to escape. Finally, the fire caught for good, and the cave began to warm up a bit.

We had an uninspired supper—dried venison and more *camas*—and after that the men promptly fell asleep.

Useless men. How could they sleep when there was a wolf lurking outside the cave? I sidled over to Jehu.

"Wake up," I whispered, nudging him.

"What?" he growled, one eye open in a squint.

"What if the wolf comes back? What if it comes back and eats us?"

Jehu flipped on his side and cuddled up to his pack, flinging his arm over it. "Don't worry, Jane. You smell too bad for any wolf to want to eat you."

I couldn't believe him. They were quite happy to sleep while some wolf was out there waiting to get back into its den? Well, I for one had no intention of being eaten by a wolf. I hauled M'Carty's rifle to my side and propped it against a wall, determined to stay awake. I stared doggedly at the entrance of the cave. The sound of the wind seemed to sing outside, lulling me, dragging me down to where it was so peaceful and warm and—

I woke abruptly, shaking my head. I had just nodded off for a moment, hadn't I? The air hummed with the soft snores of Jehu and Keer-ukso. A thin shaft of gray light streamed in through the corner of the blanket at the mouth of the cave, and I struggled to my feet, rifle in hand. I opened the blanket . . . and blinked.

Clean white snow stretched out in all directions. And it was still falling.

We were snowed in.

CHAPTER FOURTEEN
or,
Memelose Stories

The snow fell thick and fast, the wind whipping it now and then, catching it, sending it swirling through the air. We were all freezing. My calico dress and cape were no match for this weather.

Jehu's face looked grim.

"We can't just stay here," I said desperately.

"We'll die out in that snow. That's a blizzard," said Jehu. "We have enough food to last a week. If we can just hold out that long, we'll be fine. Early snow like this, I reckon it'll melt fast."

Keer-ukso nodded in agreement.

"What if it doesn't?" I whispered, terrified at the thought of being stuck in a cave in the mountains. "What if we never get out of here?"

"Then we'll die with the smell of skunk in our noses," Jehu half joked.

"This is serious, Jehu." I caught sight of pawlike indentations in the snow in front of the cave. "And what are those?" I demanded.

Keer-ukso crouched down. *"Leloo."*

Leloo? I considered for a moment. *Le loup* meant "wolf" in French. I snapped my fingers triumphantly. "Wolf!" I announced. And then went pale. "Wolf," I whispered.

"Smoke scare wolf," Keer-ukso said.

The wind shifted, blowing past me to Keer-ukso.

"Or maybe Boston Jane scare wolf," he said, wrinkling his nose.

I didn't even dignify his comment with an answer.

The morning passed slowly, marked only by the accumulation of snow. I tried to pretend that the cave was merely our parlor at home. Except, of course, it was cold and dark, reeked of skunk, and was teeming with insects.

"I can hardly believe I attended Miss Hepplewhite's Young Ladies Academy all those years to end up in a filthy cave," I muttered irritably, drawing in the dirt with a stick. I stretched and banged my head on the cave roof. "Ow."

Jehu raised an eyebrow.

"To think I had the fare for a voyage home. Which I still say I should have taken. M'Carty didn't know what he was talking about. Mr. Black was a true gentleman."

"Mr. Black, maybe he is *memelose* gentleman," Keer-ukso joked.

"Whether Black's a *memelose* or not, I don't know," said

Jehu. "But we're stuck here now, that's certain." He leaned back, stretching. "And Miss Hepplewhite can be washed out with the bilge for all I care."

I ignored him.

"I do know a thing or two about *memeloses*, you know," Jehu added mysteriously.

Keer-ukso and I both stared at Jehu, curious.

"And I can tell you the story of Fanny Neale, if you care to hear it."

Keer-ukso nodded and leaned forward. "Tell story."

"It's a true story." Jehu crossed his legs and stared into the fire. "Fanny Neale," he sighed, "was the prettiest girl on Cape Cod."

Unaccountably, I felt a twinge of irritation at the way he said her name. "Did you know her?"

"You'll have to listen and find out," he said, his eyes taunting me. "See, Fanny had this long beautiful hair, like spun silk. It was the color of gold, and it was said that if you carried one of Fanny's locks in your pocket you'd have a good sea voyage." He patted his pocket as if he carried a strand there himself.

I pictured Fanny Neale in the cave, her hair falling around her shoulders like a cape, her eyes only for Jehu.

Jehu's voice seemed to grow softer, mixing with the wind humming outside the cave. "Fanny Neale fell in love with a sailor, and they pledged their troth to each other."

I felt a peculiar clenching sensation in my chest.

"The sailor was set to ship out on a voyage, and so they

agreed that they would marry upon his return. Each day Fanny walked along the beach, looking for her beloved's ship to return.

"There was a terrible storm, and the rain battered the seas. Ship after ship was reported sunk, but Fanny Neale never lost hope. Still she walked the beach, waiting for her sailor." His voice lowered an octave, and the fire flickered. "And then one day word came that her lover's ship had sunk, and all hands were lost."

I looked into Jehu's eyes, remembering the terrible storm we had survived to arrive at Shoalwater Bay, and knew all too well how cruel fate could be. My maid, Mary, and the cabin boy, Samuel, had died during that storm.

"What happened?" Keer-ukso asked.

Jehu shook himself. "Fanny was heartbroken. She couldn't bear to live without her sailor. So she threw herself into the sea and drowned."

I gasped.

"But then, two weeks later, her sailor returned. He had managed to survive by clinging to a piece of wood. That, and the sure knowledge that his Fanny was waiting for him, kept him alive. When he found out that she had killed herself, he went down to the place where she had drowned and wept and wept. And there, on the sand, was a long thick lock of her hair, except it had turned green, become part of the sea itself."

"Seaweed," Keer-ukso whispered.

Jehu nodded. "And it's said that you can always find Fanny

Neale's hair after a storm, for she's mourning and tearing her hair out for the sailor that she lost so long ago."

The cave was quiet for a moment, and then there was a soft wailing sound on the wind, like weeping. Jehu's eyes met mine, and held. What if he were lost at sea? What would I do?

"I know *memelose* story," Keer-ukso announced, breaking the quiet.

I swallowed hard and said, "Please tell us."

"All Chinook know, very bad luck to have bones of dead person near house. And worst luck to have skull of enemy near house," Keer-ukso explained. "There was very greedy man called Kohpoh. Kohpoh wanted wife of another man. One day when Kohpoh and husband fished, Kohpoh killed husband and told woman that husband drowned. Woman cried very much and Kohpoh stayed near her. Soon, Kohpoh took woman for wife and lived in lodge of dead man."

He lowered his voice dramatically. "*Memelose* of husband come to lodge at night and sing to wife with sound of frog." And here Keer-ukso made a frog sound. "*Memelose* tell wife true story that he was killed. Tell wife to look for his skull on beach. Next morning, wife goes to beach and there is skull on sand, smiling at her." Keer-ukso placed his hands under his chin and tilted his head to the side, showing his teeth. "While Kohpoh out gambling, wife put skull under lodge."

"Then what happened?" I asked eagerly.

He arced his hand. "Terrible storm, and water came up to lodge and drag lodge into bay. And Kohpoh drowned. Next

161

morning everyone see skull on beach in same place where wife found it, and know husband had revenge."

I shivered. Hearing about a malevolent ghost was doing nothing to soothe my nerves.

"Good story," Jehu complimented. "I'll have to remember that one."

"Boston Jane, you tell *memelose* story," Keer-ukso prompted.

"Well, I do know one ghost story," I said. "I heard it when I was at Miss Hepplewhite's academy."

"This oughta be good," Jehu said, clearly trying to lighten the mood. "Wait. Don't tell me. It's a tale about a man who died from holding a fork the wrong way." He mimed stabbing himself in the heart with a fork.

"Very amusing," I said. "It's a story about a young lady called Clara. She was kind and thoughtful and obedient and good-tempered."

"Good-tempered, eh?" Jehu interrupted. "What color hair did she have?"

"I don't know. Red, I suppose."

"Sounds a lot like you."

"Oh! You're insufferable. Brown hair, then. It doesn't matter." I took a deep breath and continued. "Clara took dancing lessons from a handsome young man called Ned. Clara fell in love with Ned, and for months never dared to express her true feelings. Until one day when he arrived at lessons with a bouquet of flowers and he declared his love for her. She confessed her own affection for him, and they happily promised themselves to each other. Ned gave her a token of their secret love—a gold locket."

"Pretty good for a dancing teacher," Jehu commented.

"And she gave him a ribbon from her hair," I said. "Then one day while out walking, Clara saw Ned kissing another girl. And this other girl was wearing the very ribbon Clara had given Ned! Poor Clara was so startled that she ran straight into the middle of Chestnut Street and was struck and killed by an oncoming carriage."

Keer-ukso whistled low.

"That's not much of a ghost story," Jehu teased. "What does the ghost do? Come back and waltz?"

I ignored him. "From that day forward, Ned's life fell apart. He could hear Clara crying outside his window at night. He couldn't sleep, and his health failed. He grew haggard and pale, and one by one, he lost his students."

"She sounds like a real nag," Jehu quipped lightly, but it infuriated me.

"She was cheated by a cruel, heartless man!" I shouted.

"Finish story!" Keer-ukso ordered.

I took a deep, calming breath. "Ned started to see her everywhere he went. Finally he took to his bed and never got up."

"He died?" Jehu asked.

"Yes. And it's said that you can sometimes see the two of them dancing on Chestnut Street in the early dawn hours."

"He should have changed name. She not find him then," Keer-ukso said, nodding to himself.

"That's a terrible story," Jehu said in a disgusted voice.

"What do you mean? It's a very romantic story. She forgave him and now they're together forever," I explained.

"Sounds like a raw deal to me. Spending eternity with some nag who drove you to your death?" he mocked.

"At least it's better than marrying some man who only wants you so he can get more land!" I shot back.

"Who said anything about marriage?" Jehu said blandly.

"I wouldn't marry you if you were the last man alive! You're just as bad as William. When I marry, it shall be to a proper gentleman."

Keer-ukso's eyes flicked back and forth between us.

"A gentleman?" At this Jehu laughed coldly. "I think we are all acquainted with your good luck in finding gentlemen."

I glared at him. "Well, you're certainly not a gentleman."

"Do you think this scar on my cheek makes me no gentleman?" he demanded. "I see you staring at it all the time."

"You obviously don't understand true love," I snapped.

"You mean dying's the only way to find true love? Don't be a featherhead."

"Don't call me a featherhead!"

"I'll call you whatever I please. Who are you to order me around?" He grabbed up his pack and pushed his hat low over his eyes.

"I'm a lady and I expect to be treated as such."

"You're a smelly pest, that's what you are!"

"Well, you're a foulmouthed, ill-tempered ne'er-do-well, and I can't believe I'm stuck in a cave with you!"

"Well, you aren't!" Jehu shouted back. "Not anymore!" And with that, he grabbed M'Carty's rifle, stalked to the mouth of the cave, and without a backward glance he strode out into the storm and was swallowed up by the snow.

"Good riddance!" I shouted after him.

CHAPTER FIFTEEN
or,
Into the Wilderness

The snow fell steadily all afternoon, each flake condemning me for my ill temper.

And Jehu did not return.

"He's just doing this to spite me," I said, staring out at the snow.

"Bad luck to tell *memelose* stories," Keer-ukso said.

"No, it was bad luck for me to get dragged along on this foolish hunt!" I said, my voice strident. "Mr. Black is a gentleman. He is most certainly not a ghost bent on revenge, nor is he a murderer."

Keer-ukso sat down next to me by the fire and said, "Mr. Black, why you say he is gentleman?"

"He dressed neatly, and was well-spoken, and had very nice manners."

Keer-ukso looked thoughtful. "So does Boston William," he said, his meaning clear.

"It's not the same," I said defensively. "Mr. Black is a good man."

"Boston Jane, am I good man?"

"Of course you are."

He touched his chest. "I have no Boston suit. I not speak well."

"Keer-ukso," I said.

"Is Mr. Russell good man?"

I stared at him. "No. Mr. Russell is a filthy, ill-mannered—"

Keer-ukso interrupted. "Mr. Russell is good man. Mr. Russell, he like you, Boston Jane."

"He likes me?" I asked, astonished. "Is that why he yells at me all the time? Is that why he threw me out of the cabin into the pouring rain?"

"Yes," Keer-ukso said firmly.

The afternoon crept along slowly, like a lesson that would never end. The wilderness had turned whisper-quiet, so that every soft rustle seemed muted. I sat at the entrance of the cave and watched the snow fall in soft sheets, lacy as embroidery. It hurt my eyes to look at all of that bright snow. With each hour that passed, my unease grew until it was a tangible thing in my throat, hard and lumpy. Keer-ukso joined me at the cave entrance, watching.

"I used to like snow when I was a girl," I said with a bitter little laugh.

Keer-ukso didn't respond. He seemed so solemn and distracted, staring into the snow as if looking for something he'd

lost. His graceful profile stood out against the white background. He looked like a statue that had been carved by a sculp-
tor, his face so fine.

"I wish you'd change your name back to Handsome Jim,"
I said softly. "Keer-ukso doesn't suit you. You don't have a
crooked nose."

He didn't seem to hear me. "Oldest brother like snow." His
voice was a whisper.

"Your brother?"

He held out a hand and watched as the snow fell softly
down onto it, his fingers closing smoothly over the fluffy, fat
flakes.

"Wheeark," he said flatly. "Died long ago. *Waum sick.*"

Fever.

"Wheeark was most handsome. He always laugh at me and
say I have crooked nose." He rubbed a slight bump on his nose;
it was barely discernible. "From when I was child."

"What happened?"

Keer-ukso smiled sadly, his eyes wet. "Chase oldest brother
up tree. Then fall."

"Oh dear," I said, and gripped his hand tight. He fixed his
gaze beyond me on a thick drift of snow as if expecting to see his
brother appear and laugh and tease him about his nose.

Perhaps it was the way he was sitting—so still—that made
me want to do anything to take that grief-stricken look off his
face. Or perhaps it was that we were in the middle of the wilderness, trapped in a cave, and he was warm and smelled good to

me. Or maybe it was just because I had wanted to do it for so long.

Whatever the reason, I simply leaned forward and kissed him.

It was a strange kiss, different from Jehu's. It was softer somehow, and there was none of the electricity racing up my spine that had been there when Jehu kissed me, but still it was nice and warm and comforting in a way that felt good. It didn't seem to matter anymore that Jehu thought I was a smelly pest. Here was a man who found me pretty, who thought I was worth kissing.

For a moment Keer-ukso just sat there, kissing me back, my lips clinging to his. And then, incredibly, he moved as if someone waking from a dream, and took my shoulders and held me gently away from him.

"*Hēilo*," Keer-ukso said.

"What?"

"*No*," he said, and I was abruptly quite sick of Jargon lessons.

"But I thought—"

Pushing a tangled red curl out of my face, he said kindly, "You are good friend, Boston Jane." He clarified. "Best friend."

"A friend?"

"*Mika kahkwa ats.*"

"What's that?"

"I teach you more Jargon," he said. "*Mika* means you. *Kahkwa ats* means like sister."

"I'm like a sister to you?" I asked, astonished. "But you didn't kiss me like a sister!"

He blushed. "Like very pretty sister."

A slow, dull ache settled over my heart. Was I cursed to go through life alone? Was everyone I loved destined to die or reject me? I covered my face with my hands. I wanted to curl up into a ball and die.

"Boston Jane," Keer-ukso said softly, but I had heard enough.

"You don't understand!" I shouted in frustration, tears springing to my eyes. "William wanted me for the land, and you think I'm a sister, and Jehu, Jehu—"

And Jehu doesn't even want me anymore! I wanted to cry but didn't.

A wolf's soulful bark echoed in the rapidly falling darkness.

"Jehu," I whispered, but his name was snatched away by the wind.

Darkness descended on the mountain, and with it a thick gloom that seemed to fill the very air.

Still Jehu did not return.

"Sleep," Keer-ukso urged, wrapping a blanket over my shoulders.

I shook my head. No, I couldn't fall asleep. A feeling of dread as thick as the skunk smell had entered the cave. I knew that if I fell asleep, he would never come back. That Jehu was lost out there in the snowstorm and he would die. And that my harsh, foolish words had been the last thing he heard from my lips.

Just as it had been with Papa.

The night dragged on. The snow tapered off, and the stars emerged to blink high in the heavens. Had it really just been a few months ago that Jehu and I had danced under a starry sky so much like this one? If I strained my ears, I could almost hear the sound of the fiddle rising in the night air, see Jehu's blue eyes glittering down at me full of laughter and warmth and something more, something I recognized at the time but couldn't bear to admit.

He was a sailor, his personality so intertwined with the sea that even his hair smelled like a salty breeze. But why had he turned his back on it? Abandoned a life he loved, to stay in this wretched wilderness?

For you, a small voice inside me whispered.

I suddenly knew that he didn't want to marry me to get land. That I had been horribly, horribly wrong. I closed my eyes and remembered the proud look in his eye when Mrs. Frink offered him her crumble cake.

I'll have a piece of pie. Jane makes wonderful pie, he'd said warmly, his eyes settling on mine with simple conviction.

He had come back for me. He had stayed for me.

Me, Jane Peck.

And I had driven him away with my cruel words.

Another horrible thought occurred to me. If I had been wrong about Jehu, had I been wrong about other people? Like Mr. Russell?

Mr. Russell, he like you, Keer-ukso had said. I looked over at him now where he lay huddled by the fire, snoring softly.

All at once I remembered lying in the bunk in Mr. Russell's cabin, so sunk into myself that I couldn't hear anything but my own grief beating against my head. And then there was his voice dragging me back from that dark place.

You hear me, gal? I said ya stink!

I hadn't heard it then, but I heard it now. The worry. The concern.

The mountain man hadn't been trying to hurt or humiliate me. No, he had bullied me back to life. He had dragged me kicking and screaming back from the edge of despair and dropped me on the porch in the cold rain because he cared about me. Because beneath that filthy, grizzled, uncivilized exterior was a good man. A good man who spat far too much tobacco and could stand to bathe once in a while, but a good man all the same.

Mr. Black's face rose up before me, a menacing shadow.

I have some unfinished business up this way. Loose ends to tie up, you might say.

And I had sent him after Mr. Russell, I realized, a lump of anguish sticking in my throat. It was all suddenly too much. I couldn't take it. Papa was dead. Jehu was probably dead. And Mr. Russell would be dead soon, too. And nothing would bring them back. Not good manners, or a thousand cups of perfectly poured tea. They were gone forever and I had realized too late what truly mattered.

Or had I?

I looked out into the cold, black night. The wind had died down and a bright moon illuminated the glittering snow.

Jehu was out there, somewhere.

I felt something stiffen deep in my soul, and I grabbed up my walking stick, tugging my cape tight around me.

Then I headed into the wilderness.

CHAPTER SIXTEEN
or,
A Girl like Jane

The moon was brighter than any torch, and I walked for what felt like hours, ignoring the cold and my freezing feet. Where could he have gone? The falling snow had obliterated his trail. It was small comfort that he had taken the rifle.

As the night tripped on, I began to lose hope, and by the time the pale dawn light was kissing the horizon I was frantic. I called Jehu's name, shouting it to the very trees as if they might be kind enough to let me know which direction to take. My footsteps left a clear trail, so I knew I would be able to find my way back to the cave.

"Je-hu!" I called. "Je-hu!"

Sometimes it seemed as if I heard a voice answer, echoing back to me on the cold, chill air.

In the end it was not my cries that found Jehu, but my foot. I tripped right over him.

He was buried in a thick drift of snow, and only his hat was visible. I crawled next to him, digging him out as quickly as I could.

"Jane," he croaked hoarsely, his face pale.

"Are you hurt?"

"My leg."

There was a long, ragged gash cut through the pant. I felt my way along the leg as Papa had taught me, but I could find no break. Still, it was swelling fast, and he would quite likely have difficulty walking. I tore a length of fabric off my skirt and proceeded to wrap the leg.

"I was getting mighty tired of dried venison. Thought a little roasted rabbit might be tasty. So I set off after this rabbit, and then the ground just gave way beneath me and I went tumbling. Crawled back up here," he said, leaning his head against my chest, his eyes fluttering shut.

"No, Jehu," I said, shaking him awake. "You can't fall asleep."

His eyes opened a slit.

"Can you stand?" I demanded.

He opened his mouth to speak, and then his eyes went wide in warning. I snatched the rifle from his frozen fingers, whirling around to protect him with my very life.

A familiar large, lumpy figure stood outlined by the rising sun.

"Hairy Bill!" I exclaimed with, I confess, delight.

"Ma'am," he said, tipping his furry hat.

"Guess you were right about him following us," Jehu joked tiredly, his eyes shutting again.

"Hurry," I urged Hairy Bill. "We must get him back to the cave."

Supporting him between us, we managed to half carry, half drag Jehu back to the cave, one leg tied with a bloody rag, his face pale and drawn. Keer-ukso saw us trudging up the pass and ran down to us. He grasped Jehu's hand.

"Brought some rabbit for breakfast," Jehu whispered.

"Rabbit?"

Jehu smiled weakly, and pointed to his sack.

Keer-ukso slapped Jehu's back in admiration.

I made Jehu comfortable and then prepared roast rabbit for breakfast.

Jehu, who had warmed up by this point and was feeling better with some food in his belly, animatedly described his adventures. After we had finished our breakfast, Keer-ukso and Hairy Bill headed out to survey the vicinity to see if the snow was melting enough for us to continue our journey.

Jehu, his cheeks flush from the fire, his thick black curls plastered to his forehead, his scar winking up at me, fell asleep where he was sitting against the cave wall.

I took off my cape and tucked it high under his chin.

And breathed again.

In the late afternoon the sun burst out from behind its gray shield. The snow rapidly turned into wet, heavy slush.

The swelling had gone down in Jehu's leg, but I thought it better that he not walk on it, at least for this day. Hairy Bill and

Keer-ukso rigged a litter that they dragged along. As we made our way down the mountain, the slush gave way to deep squishy mud that caught at my boots and tugged at my skirts. Then it began to rain.

In addition to being muddy and smelling of skunk, my skirt was soon soaked, and my petticoats chafed my skin until it was raw. Only Hairy Bill seemed to keep dry in his amazing cape. We walked for an eternity, and finally the rain tapered off. But every step in my thick, wet petticoats made my legs feel like lead. Soon the men and the litter were far ahead of me. They rounded a bend, and when I went round it they were nowhere in sight! Had they left me behind?

Despairing, I sat down on a fallen log. I was in the middle of the wilderness with nothing but wild animals and foul weather, and I had been abandoned. I was going to die here, and nobody would ever find me because they'd have to dig through so much mud to get to the girl—

"Jane."

I looked up, swallowing hard. Jehu and Keer-ukso and Hairy Bill were all crowded around me.

"Are you okay?" Jehu asked, a strange expression on his face.

"No!" I wailed. "I'm soaking wet, my skirts are muddy, I smell like a skunk, and I'm going to die here in the wilderness!"

"Your hair looks real curly, though," he said with a gentle smile, fingering a thick wet strand.

"Take off skirt," Keer-ukso said.

"Take off my skirt? Are you mad?"

He pointed to the thick layers of petticoats. "Too heavy." He patted his own pack. "Wear Boston pants."

"Wear a man's pants? But I'm a lady!" I said hoarsely.

"You're too pretty for anyone to mistake you for a man," Jehu said.

Keer-ukso's eyes seemed to agree with Jehu, and I bit my lip. I supposed no one would see us in the wilderness. See *me*, I amended. My gaze slipped to Hairy Bill, who was looking at me expectantly.

"I'm not going to change in front of you!" I said.

"Don't mind me, gal," Hairy Bill leered.

"You," I ordered Hairy Bill, "go as far away as possible. And you two," I said, pointing at Jehu and Keer-ukso, "watch him to make sure he doesn't get lost and wander back."

"Well, I never," Hairy Bill muttered. "I'm a married man."

Keer-ukso dug out the pants and handed them to me, and I went behind a bush. I peeled the soaking wet skirts off. My legs were raw from where the wet fabric had chafed at them. I quickly slipped into the pants. They were huge but blessedly dry. At least they matched my boy's boots, although I hardly thought that the young ladies back in Philadelphia would be rushing out to purchase the ensemble.

"Quite fetching," Jehu said when I emerged.

"Oh please," I huffed, clutching the huge waist.

"They're a bit big." He pulled a piece of rope out of his bag and looped it around my waist, his fingers moving fast, expertly knotting. Jehu winked at me. "This'll keep 'em up."

"I certainly hope so," I muttered. "The world is not ready to see Jane Peck in her unmentionables."

Jehu chuckled.

I began to fold up my skirt. It was a sodden, stinking bundle.

"You're not carrying that with you?" Jehu asked askance.

Even Keer-ukso groaned.

"Of course I am. After I wash it, it shall be as good as new. I am not about to show up at this get-together dressed like a man! What will the governor think?"

"Who cares what he thinks? That skirt stinks to high heaven."

"I'll carry it. I don't mind the smell," I said, shoving the mess into my pack.

"That's 'cause the rest of you smells just like it," he muttered.

I was exhausted, every muscle aching, when we finally stopped for the night. I rather doubted we'd even walked a mile because of the mud and slush. We camped at the bottom of the mountain, not far from a river that roared and crashed in the distance like an angry child.

I collapsed on a blanket of somewhat dry pine needles, tugging off my boots. My feet were throbbing.

"I didn't know that feet could hurt so much," I groaned.

"You haven't spent enough time on 'em," Hairy Bill said with a grunt.

"When are we going to get there?" I begged Keer-ukso. I feared that between the lost canoe, the snowstorm, and Jehu's injured leg we were making very poor progress. "What if we're too late? What if Mr. Black gets there first?"

Jehu's head snapped up. "You're worried about Black getting Russell?"

I folded my hands and looked down. "I've had some time to think, and I believe that, perhaps, Mr. Black might have ill intentions toward Mr. Russell," I said in a careful voice.

"I'm gone for one day and look what happens!" Jehu shook his head and whistled low. "What brought on this change of heart?"

"Nothing," I said stiffly. "I just had time to think."

He eyed me closely. "C'mon, Jane."

I stared at him.

"Well?"

"I saw his back," I mumbled.

"You saw his back? You mean his bare back?"

I nodded shortly.

He folded his arms, his lips set in a line. "Well, well, well."

I flushed hotly. "It's not what you think."

"I can think of a lot of things."

"It was foggy. Anyway, he was taking a bath and I saw his back—"

He raised an eyebrow.

"He was taking a bath," I continued. "Something you could stand to do yourself!"

"Least I don't smell like skunk."

"Ooof! I wish you *had* frozen to death! Then maybe I could finish a sentence properly."

"It's all about 'properly' with you. What's so proper about watching a man take a bath? That something you learned at that fancy school of yours?" he drawled.

"I was fetching water and he was at the stream and I saw his—"

"Bare back," Jehu supplied helpfully.

"And it was covered with terrible, terrible scars!" I finished on a screech.

Jehu was silent for a moment. He and Keer-ukso exchanged a meaningful look.

Keer-ukso pressed his lips together and nodded. "Probably not *memelose*," he said thoughtfully.

After a restless night haunted by dreams of Mr. Black's inscrutable face, I awoke early, tired and wrung out.

It had rained again sometime during the night, but now the sun was peeking its pink head over the trees like a curious kitten. A man's snoring rumbled in my ear. Keer-ukso was sprawled out, fast asleep an arm's length away from me, but both Hairy Bill and Jehu were gone.

Had Mr. Black set upon us during the night? Had he kidnapped Jehu and Hairy Bill at gunpoint while we slept? Was he picking us off one by one, just as he'd done with the rest of the Silencers?

A snatch of song whispered through the morning air, elusive as the wind.

Mr. Black?

I took a deep breath and set out carefully, creeping low. The song became louder as I got closer to the river.

I peered through the bushes—and could hardly believe my eyes.

Jehu was kneeling by the river, my skirt in hand, scrubbing it against the rocks as he hummed a sea tune.

He was washing my skirt!

For a moment all I could do was watch him as he scrubbed my filthy skirt in the river. It was the most beautiful sight I'd ever seen. He stood ankle deep in the water, his black hair gleaming in the sunlight like a crow's wing. He slapped and banged and rinsed my skirt again and again, holding it up to smell it every few minutes, pulling back with a grimace each time. My heart swelled so full with love I thought it might burst—and then it nearly stopped beating.

For ambling lazily up along the riverbank was a grizzly bear, headed right for Jehu!

It was clear to see that I was going to have to rescue him again.

I bolted out of my hiding place, shouting loudly to get the bear's attention. "Oh hello! Pardon me!" I shouted to the bear.

The bear paused and looked at me, as if curious. And then its head went down and it started to lope on again.

I grabbed up a rock the size of my palm and threw it with all my might at the bear.

"Jane—no!" I heard Jehu shout.

The rock bounced off the bear's head, and it turned on me with a roar.

"Run, Jane!"

I ran up along the river, the bear growling behind me. I dearly hoped Jehu had the rifle with him. For by the roaring of the bear, it was plain to me that an apology, however well-intentioned, would not suffice.

Ahead of me, the riverbank narrowed to a cliff.

"Hang on, Jane!" Jehu hollered, limping as fast as he could on his injured leg.

I paused on the edge of the cliff, looking back. I could see Jehu in the distance scrambling up after the bear, but he was still quite far. The bear, however, was steps away from me. It shook its head and roared at me, advancing at a terrible pace, its teeth sharp and snarling. I looked at Jehu and back at the bear and then did the only thing one could do in such unfortunate circumstances.

I jumped, of course.

While I had not given the present situation much study, I was well aware of my history of bad luck when it came to cliffs and rivers. I had fallen off a cliff during the summer and had nearly drowned trying to rescue a canoe from a river. It seemed to me that the most sensible way to avoid such predicaments was to steer clear of cliffs and rivers. I considered all of this as I went tumbling through the air, the landscape a blur, the colors bright around me, the sound of Jehu's shouting a soft note in the background.

When I hit the icy water, the breath left my body.

My head bobbed up, and I opened my mouth and sucked in great gulps of air as the current swept me away.

I was traveling fast down the river and I was freezing cold, but I felt amazingly calm. Perhaps I was getting used to putting my life in danger. Still, it seemed very silly to think of drowning on such a beautiful day. The sun was shining and the sky was the bright blue that always came after a storm, and come to think of it, it wasn't really all that terrible a way to die. Drowning certainly seemed a kinder way to end one's days than being eaten by a grizzly bear.

"Jane!"

Jehu was shouting at me from the riverbank, and the next thing I knew, he had dived into the river, and I felt a strong arm around my waist tugging me toward shore. He shoved me up on the bank and I lay there, breathing hard.

Jehu grabbed me by my upper arms, pulling me to my feet and shaking me.

"What were you thinking?" he demanded furiously.

"I—I—" I said, gasping for breath, holding him tight.

"You are the most foolish girl I've ever met in my entire life!"

"I saved your life!" I shouted. "And I'm tired of being bossed around by a bunch of men! I'm wet and muddy and I stink and I'm sick of everything!"

"Oh, Jane," he said, his face softening. "You may be muddy. And you may be wet. And you may smell like a skunk, but you're still the bravest girl I've ever known."

I held my breath.

He gently moved a wet hunk of hair off my nose and looked into my eyes. "There's never been a girl quite like you, Jane."

All I could do was stare at him, stunned.

What did a young lady say to such a pronouncement? What would Miss Hepplewhite recommend in such a situation? Or Mrs. Frink for that matter? Truly what should I do when confronted with a sailor whose eyes had haunted my dreams for so long that I saw them in the blue of the sky after a hard rain . . . except maybe kiss him?

And that's just what I did.

Afterward Jehu denied that he had ever been in any danger.

"I saved your life! That bear was definitely going to kill you, just like the grizzly that got Mr. Black," I said as we walked along the trail, his hand warmly clasping mine. "You didn't see the look in its eyes."

"That bear," Jehu said, tweaking my nose affectionately, "was minding its own business until you threw that rock at him." He paused importantly, slinging my wet skirt over his shoulder with a slap. "And for the record, I saved you from drowning."

"You did not! I was doing perfectly fine on my own."

"Perfectly fine drowning, I'd say," Jehu guffawed. "I saved your life."

I looked at his dear face—his laughing eyes, his scarred cheek, his dancing grin—and knew that we were both right.

In the end, we had saved each other.

CHAPTER SEVENTEEN
or,
The Rendezvous

Hairy Bill had vanished.

And we soon discovered that our rifle had, too.

"Oh!" I said, stomping my feet in fury, wet and shivering. "How could he leave us unarmed in the wilderness? If I ever see that man again—"

Jehu waved a scrap of hide. "Maybe you will. He left this."

I looked at the scrap. It said:

IOU ONE RIFLE. H.B.

I confess, I was astonished that the man could write.

After we spent the better part of the morning huddled in blankets and drying our wet clothes by the fire, Jehu urged me to pack, insisting that we continue on.

"I've barely recovered from being mauled by that grizzly bear," I complained.

"That bear," he said with a grim look, "wasn't a grizzly."

"How do you know?"

He took me by the hand and led me some distance from where we had camped.

"Because *that* is a grizzly," he said, pointing at a huge, still corpse on the ground.

The dead bear was massive, at least twice as tall as the one that had chased after me, and its head was riddled with bullet holes. I gripped Jehu and leaned forward to get a better look. And then jerked back in shock.

One of its paws had been hacked off.

By midday we spotted a group of people in the distance.

Keer-ukso broke into a grin as he recognized the party. "My friends!"

It was a group of Chehalis Indians, and as it turned out, they were also headed to the rendezvous. Keer-ukso greeted the party happily and immediately disappeared with another young man.

They were very kind and lent us a horse so that Jehu's leg would have an opportunity to heal. In spite of the warm welcome we received from the tribe, I was feeling very agitated. The closer we came to the rendezvous point, the more nervous I became. What if Mr. Black was already there? It seemed clear he wasn't a ghost, but I had one nagging worry. Why hadn't he eaten anything?

I finally gave voice to my fears as we trekked along.

"I cooked him supper, and he didn't eat a bite. Not even the pie!" I confessed.

Jehu cracked a small grin. "That just makes him a fool, Jane. Not a ghost."

Far ahead of us, I saw Keer-ukso eyeing a young woman. She seemed not the least bit interested in him, a rather unusual occurrence, considering the moonfaced girls who generally trailed after him.

"Say he is a man, and not a ghost. What do we do then?"

Jehu gazed at me steadily. "We stop him, of course."

"He has a gun, Jehu. I saw it."

"I'm sure he does. But so does every other man in the territory. Russell's no fool. I gave him that letter myself, so he knows this fellow's coming after him. I'm sure he's got his ears open. Plus we have an advantage."

"What?"

He looked around. "How about all these Indians at our back?"

Jehu's confidence did little to calm my fears.

At dusk we neared the summit of a low hill. Spread out before us was the Chehalis River, and along it an encampment of tents. When I saw the broad, flat expanse of river, I was overcome with despair, berating myself for having lost the canoe.

Jehu must have read the expression on my face for he said, "Don't feel bad, Jane. It doesn't connect to the bay. We would have had to walk anyway."

With a shout, the young men in our party took off at a run, racing to be the first to reach the encampment.

I grinned up at Jehu, bolstered by the men's good spirits.

"Hyak cooley!" I gestured wildly to Keer-ukso.

We raced down the hill and dived into the crowd of Indians. Decked out in their best clothes were representatives from tribes all along the southwest portion of the territory. Massive rough-hewn wooden tables were weighted down with food: geese, and deer, and elk, and large bundles of fresh-caught fish. The irresistible smell of biscuits and roasted potatoes made our mouths water as Jehu, Keer-ukso, and I worked our way through the bustling throng.

Here and there were the sounds of angry, raised voices, and the air hummed with the Jargon. Shouting and gunshots punctuated the night. Altogether, it reminded me a great deal of the raucous Fourth of July celebration on Shoalwater Bay, except there was enough food for a month.

I pushed my way through a phalanx of men and saw Mr. Russell deep in conversation with Mr. Swan.

"Mr. Russell!" I shouted.

Mr. Russell looked up in surprise as I flung myself at him.

"My dear?" Mr. Swan said in surprise.

"You're alive!" I shouted, hugging the mountain man happily. He was alive! Relief washed over me.

"Course I'm alive," Mr. Russell said, yanking away from me, clearly made uncomfortable by my embrace. "What are ya doing here, gal? Who's milking Bertie?" Mr. Russell asked in a sharp voice.

"Mr. Black is after you!"

He blinked. "Who?"

"Mr. Abraham Black! He came through the settlement. He's coming to kill you."

Jehu shoved forward, Keer-ukso right behind him. "We know all about it. M'Carty told us," I went on.

"What are you talking about, my dear?" Mr. Swan asked in a curious voice.

"Mr. Black, he wants to kill you," Keer-ukso added.

"I don't know anyone called Black," Mr. Russell said with a shrug.

"Yes, but M'Carty said that Mr. Black was after you, and that he would kill you if he caught you!"

Mr. Swan and Mr. Russell exchanged a glance. "Had M'Carty been"—here Mr. Swan gestured as if tipping a glass—"had M'Carty been imbibing?"

"Yes, but it was just whiskey," I said, recalling the nearly empty bottle.

"My dear," Mr. Swan began. "M'Carty has a habit of . . . how do I say this?" He cleared his throat loudly. "He has a habit of conjuring up tales when he is imbibing whiskey."

"But he didn't make it up! I saw Mr. Black!" I insisted.

Mr. Russell didn't seem the least bit concerned. "Told ya, gal, I don't know any fella named Black."

"But you must! We traveled so far and we got caught in the mountains and a bear chased me and I nearly drowned and now you mean to tell me that you don't even know Mr. Black?" I shouted. I was so vexed I wanted to kill the man myself.

"Yep," Mr. Russell said in a laconic voice, gray whiskers twitching. He spit a huge wad of tobacco.

"But you were a fur trapper, weren't you?"

"Yep."

"And you trapped for the Rocky Mountain Fur Company?"

"Yep."

"Then you know about the Silencers!"

"Silencers?"

"Yes," I hissed. "The other men you trapped with! The Silencers."

Mr. Russell chomped on his tobacco for a moment. "I trapped alone, gal. Didn't trap with no one else."

Jehu and Keer-ukso and I shared a skeptical look.

"But M'Carty said—"

"My dear," Mr. Swan interjected smoothly. "I do believe M'Carty has filled your ears with some very tall tales." A rifle was fired loudly quite near us and we all flinched. A moment later the distinct sound of a brawl broke out.

"What's going on here?" Jehu asked.

Mr. Swan looked very harried. "I'm rather afraid the negotiations are not going very well at all. As you can see, there are representatives from all the tribes in the area in attendance. It's been a rather lengthy affair, as the governor has been obliged to speak the terms of the treaty in English, which are then translated into the Jargon, and then into the individual languages of all the tribes."

"And the terms of the treaty?" I asked.

"The Indians are to sell them their land, and then they are all to move onto one designated reservation."

"For what?" Keer-ukso asked flatly.

"A fee for the land, paid in installments, as well as the government's promise to supply carpenters, blacksmiths, a school, a doctor, a sawmill, and farming equipment. There would be no liquor permitted, and the Indians would be allowed to come and go as they pleased from the reservation," Mr. Swan explained. "Which, in some cases, unfortunately means that Indians shall be obliged to move away from land where they've lived forever."

Keer-ukso snorted at this point. "Why leave ancestors' graves? Why live with all tribes on reservation? Everyone will fight."

Mr. Swan smiled weakly. "That is exactly what everyone is objecting to, my dear fellow. A Chehalis *tyee* named Tleyuk didn't think this was fair at all."

Keer-ukso nodded. "I know Tleyuk."

"It became even more complicated," Swan went on, "when the governor reluctantly acknowledged that even after the Indians signed the treaty, it would have to be sent back to Washington for approval."

"I see their point," Jehu said. "If he doesn't have any real authority to negotiate with them, why should they bother?"

"Yes, well, I'm afraid it all came to a head when Tleyuk's father, who had retired as *tyee* because of his weakness for liquor, got his hands on some whiskey," Mr. Swan finished lamely.

"Or was given it," Mr. Russell growled.

"It seems to be a weakness of many men in the territory," I said, raising an eyebrow pointedly.

Mr. Swan's cheeks reddened, but he soldiered on. "Anyway, Tleyuk's father began mumbling some rather incoherent support for his son, and the governor lost his temper and began yelling at the old man to sit down, and then everyone started shouting and it all fell apart. Tleyuk was the angriest of all because the governor had promised that there was to be no liquor at the meeting. He accused the governor of getting his father drunk on purpose. He said that the governor was probably just going to put all the Indians on ships and send them north, and that the governor could no longer be trusted."

"That sounds like something your old friend William would suggest," Jehu said dryly.

"Tleyuk is smart," Keer-ukso agreed.

Mr. Swan patted his forehead with a handkerchief. "Tleyuk is also very charismatic, and now he is refusing to sign the treaty. It's been chaos ever since the negotiations broke up. It's quite likely that the other tribes shall follow Tleyuk. I do believe the governor is in for some trouble."

"What happens now?" Jehu asked.

There was a flurry of fighting nearby, and what looked to be one of the governor's men went sprawling headfirst into the dirt. We stepped away.

"If we survive the night, I imagine we get back to negotiations. Although it does appear to be a capital mess at the moment." Mr. Swan yawned. "I do believe I'll turn in. Coming, Mr. Russell?"

194

Mr. Russell grunted and followed him, deftly avoiding a fly-ing chicken leg.

We watched as the two men disappeared into the throng.

"Do you believe Mr. Russell?" I asked, dumbfounded.

Jehu shook his head as if to clear it. "I don't know what to believe."

Keer-ukso said, "Mr. Russell, he is not scared."

"You're right about that. If I had a murderer on my tail, I'd look a lot more worried. And M'Carty *had* been drinking because of his leg," Jehu mused.

"For many days," Keer-ukso said in agreement.

"But what about Mr. Black's scarred back?" I asked. "I saw it."

"You said it was kind of foggy, though, right?"

"Yes, well, I suppose it was foggy, but I know what I saw."

Jehu sighed. "We have to take him at his word."

"I can't believe this," I said to no one in particular.

"At least Mr. Russell is not dead," Keer-ukso observed.

"Not yet, at least," I said darkly.

"Jane," Jehu said, "the man has no reason to lie."

"I suppose you're right," I admitted. Indeed, Mr. Russell did not seem the least bit perturbed. The only thing he had seemed upset about was that I had abandoned his precious cow.

After the best supper I'd had in days, I collapsed, sleeping restlessly because of all the noise and fighting. The next morn-ing, as I was pouring a cup of coffee, a voice I knew all too well said, "Jane."

"William," I answered flatly.

"You're looking . . . ," he said, his eyes raking over my outfit, pausing on my long, loose, tangled hair, "well."

I was immediately aware of my travel-worn outfit. My hand went to my hair to tame it, and once again I felt like the unpolished eleven-year-old girl who had been so eager to impress and bend and please a man she worshipped. I forced myself to put my hand at my side.

"What brings you here?" he asked.

I could hardly tell him the real reason, so I improvised. "I was delivering a very important communication to Mr. Swan."

He seemed amused by this. "Really?"

"How are the negotiations going?" I challenged.

"They are going as well as can be expected when negotiating with savages," he said in a dismissive voice. He sighed in a world-weary way. "It seems that it will take some time. One of the savages is particularly tiresome, and a troublemaker as well. I have advised the governor to take him firmly in hand before his mutiny spreads."

Maybe he doesn't like being bossed around by an egotistical man! I wanted to shout, but I just stared at him.

"Jane, perhaps you should find somewhere to clean up. You must be embarrassed to be seen by everyone as you are," William said abruptly. "If you run along to my tent, you can ask my wife for some suitable clothes."

I couldn't help but think that his gray eyes, which I had once so admired, greatly resembled dishwater. How had I ever thought him handsome?

"Jehu was right," I blurted. *"Mika kahkwa pelton."*

You are a fool.

"What did you say?"

"Oh sorry, I forgot that you don't understand the Jargon," I said in an innocent voice.

His face reddened.

Mr. Swan appeared as if summoned. "My dear," he asked, pulling me aside gently. "Would you please go find Mr. Russell? The negotiations are ready to resume."

"Of course," I said, eager to be as far away from William Baldt as possible.

"Capital. I believe he was cleaning the breakfast dishes in the stream over yonder, behind the tents."

I practically ran in the direction of the stream, crashing through the thick woods. Who did William Baldt think he was to criticize me? The man was positively infuriating. And besides, Jehu liked my hair just the way it was!

I was so lost in thought that I almost screamed when I heard the soft voice whisper through the trees.

"Obediah."

The whole landscape went still, the birds' chirping fading in some strange muted way so that the only sound I heard was the soft wind blowing. I crept forward in the direction of the voice and saw Mr. Russell at the edge of the stream, hands frozen over a tin plate.

Mr. Black was standing behind him, his hand casually resting on the butt of his pistol.

"You're looking older, Obediah," Mr. Black said. "Your hair's gone gray."

Mr. Russell's shoulders sagged in weary acceptance, as if he had been expecting this for a long time. He turned around, his face lined and tired. He looked like an old man. "We're both a lot older, Abe."

"That we are." Mr. Black rubbed the handle of his gun. "Well then. I reckon you know why I'm here."

"Reckon I do," Mr. Russell replied in a defeated voice. His left hand was shaking. "Mind if I finish with the rest of these?" he asked, holding up a dirty tin plate.

Mr. Black shrugged. "Don't see as if it'll make any difference. Go on ahead."

I watched in suspense as Mr. Russell proceeded to clean the rest of the plates while Mr. Black stood by patiently, like an executioner waiting for the condemned to finish a last meal. After a few minutes there was a neat pile of clean plates.

"I'm finished," Mr. Russell said, standing up and wiping his hands on his pants.

"Might as well get on with it, then," Mr. Black said.

"Might as well."

Mr. Black drew his gun, and Mr. Russell stared stubbornly down at the ground. He was just going to stand there and let Mr. Black shoot him?

"Stop!" I shouted, rushing out of the trees and in front of Mr. Russell.

Mr. Black looked startled. "Miss Peck?"

"Gal?" Mr. Russell said in a shocked voice.

"You can't kill Mr. Russell!"

"Gal, get on out of here," Mr. Russell said, shoving me away.

"No!" I whispered fiercely.

"Miss Peck, I have no quarrel with you. None at all. But I've traveled a long way to put a bullet between that man's eyes, and I'm not leaving until I do just that."

Mr. Russell went white.

"You can't kill Mr. Russell!" I said.

"I'm a good enough shot that I can hit him between the eyes even with you standing there," he said simply.

"But he's a good man!"

"Good man? Do you have any idea what this good man did, my dear young lady?" he asked with a grim laugh.

"No," I said through the thick undercurrent of menace. Anything to keep him talking. Keep him from shooting Mr. Russell.

"This good man," he said in a mocking voice, "left me to rot after a grizzly ripped my back off like it was a piece of hide. This man took my food, my horse, my gear, and left me to die." He laughed low, a mean laugh. "Except, I didn't die. Bet you didn't count on that, eh, Obediah? I know Toby, and Elijah, and Jack were real surprised to see me walking and breathing. Why, I didn't even have to put a bullet through Toby—he just plumb dropped dead when he saw me standing there." He gave a spooky grin. "Thought I was a ghost."

Mr. Russell flinched as if struck.

"But I'm no dead man. See, I was born again on that mountain, Miss Peck, and I've got the scars to prove it." His eyes narrowed. "But then again, I think you already know that."

"Please," I whispered. "You must believe that they never would have left you there if they thought you were alive. They truly believed you were dead!"

He laughed harshly. "Believe me, Miss Peck," he said, his eyes still locked with Mr. Russell's, "when I woke up I wished I was dead." His face went dark in remembered pain. "For the first couple of hours I screamed for him, I screamed for them all. But they were gone. Long gone. Don't know how long I laid there, my back festering from where that bear had clawed me."

I held my breath.

"Do you know what I had to do?" he asked matter-of-factly, as if we were having a polite conversation.

"What?"

"I crawled, Miss Peck. I crawled for an entire day to get from where you're standing to where I stand, and then I scraped the grubs from under a rotten log and laid on them. You ever sleep in a pile of grubs, Miss Peck?"

I wanted to say that Sleeping in Grubs was not part of the curriculum at the Young Ladies Academy, but didn't think he'd appreciate my joke.

"Those grubs saved my life. Ate out the infection. But that was just the beginning. See, I still couldn't walk, and they hadn't left me any food, and they took my gear, so I survived for months on berries and bugs and tree bark. Whatever I could get to, crawling on my elbows. I don't believe I'll ever get the taste of tree bark out of my mouth." He swallowed hard at that memory.

This was perfectly awful. I could practically taste the bark myself.

"By the time I reached the fort months later, my clothes had rotted away and I looked like a skeleton. That's what the boy who found me thought I was. He screamed when he saw me." He looked blankly at Mr. Russell. "I crawled the whole way, Obediah. Crawled two hundred miles through Indian country without even a knife."

He paused, looking up at the sky.

"Took me nearly five months to be able to walk again. But that wasn't even the worst of it. No," he said, shaking his head. "The worst was finding out that my dear Lucinda, my only reason for living, was gone because this man here"—he punctuated the words by stabbing his pistol at Mr. Russell—"told her I was dead."

"Abe," Mr. Russell said.

"Not a word," he said in a voice cold as death itself. "You killed her just as surely as if you'd shot her through the heart. You just walked up and killed my Lucinda. I can forgive you for the rest, but I can't never forgive you for that."

Mr. Russell sighed in resignation.

"Now you go on and move away, Miss Peck," Mr. Black said, waving his gun. "You're a good girl. But you should've taken my advice and gone back home."

"You don't understand!" I said desperately.

"I understand that I'm gonna shoot Obediah."

"This man saved my life!" I burst out.

In the distance I heard the shouting of voices as the negotiations began.

"What do you mean, he saved your life?" Mr. Black asked in a deceptively quiet voice.

"When I found out that Papa had died, I wanted to die. I took to my bed in the cabin and refused to get up."

Mr. Black stood motionless.

"I wanted to die," I said passionately, "just like your Lucinda. You see, I couldn't bear the thought of living in a world without Papa. I couldn't bear the thought of being alone." I twisted my hands. "I—I—stopped eating and—" Here I felt the old despair well up in me for a brief moment. "And everyone tried to help me, I know they did. But I was determined and . . . "

"And then?" Mr. Black said in a voice devoid of emotion.

I looked into his impenetrable eyes. "But Mr. Russell was more determined that I should live. He made me get out of bed. He saved my life," I finished quietly.

Mr. Black didn't lower his gun. "So how's that change anything?"

"This, this"—I confess I almost said *filthy* man!—"this noble man is my family!" I declared earnestly. "He is all the family I know. If you kill him, you will be killing the only family I have." I paused. "And me with him, because I tell you I cannot bear to lose another person."

Mr. Russell held his breath.

"I beg you, please. Whatever wrong was committed to you was done by another man, a younger man, and he is not the same man. He has suffered and paid for his sins. You said I reminded you of another lady. Was it your wife? Was it Lucinda?"

Mr. Black nodded mutely. "She had hair the exact shade as yours," he said, his voice thick with grief.

"Then please," I begged, "in her memory, spare his life. She would not want his blood on your hands."

The gun was shaking in his hand, his face working with unnamed emotions.

"She was my friend, too, Abe," Mr. Russell said huskily, his eyes wet.

Mr. Russell and Mr. Black just stood there, staring across the clearing, seeing each other as they truly were: two old men whose lives had been twisted by sorrow and anger and regret.

A warm breeze filled the air, a breeze so sweet that it tasted like sunshine or laughter or maybe just hope. We lifted our faces to it, letting it brush across our skin and fill our senses, like the elusive perfume of a vibrant red-haired woman who has left the room.

And I thought that perhaps Mr. Black remembered. Remembered what it had been like when nothing had stood between him and Mr. Russell, when they had been each other's best friend and truest companion. That, for a brief moment, the years fell away and all that was left were two brash young men— flush with excitement, bound by friendship—standing there looking at each other as they had so many years ago, ready to embark on a grand adventure.

Mr. Black sighed heavily and lowered his gun, rubbing his forehead.

I breathed a great sigh of relief.

But then Mr. Black looked up, his eyes dark and full of terrible purpose. He raised his arm, aimed his gun straight at us, and cocked it.

I squeezed my eyes shut in horror.

And heard the cocking of what seemed a hundred guns.

I opened my eyes a squint.

Jehu was holding a rifle to Mr. Black's head, his eyes fixed firmly on me.

All around the clearing, men stood with their rifles pointed at Mr. Black: Keer-ukso, Mr. Swan, Chief Toke, Indians from other tribes, even William Baldt. They held their rifles steadily, their meaning clear, but still Mr. Black pointed his gun at Mr. Russell for a long, heart-stopping moment.

"My good fellow, you're a wanted man," Mr. Swan declared loudly, his voice shaking. "You really ought to be moving along."

Jehu nudged Mr. Black with the barrel of his rifle. "Leave your gun while you're at it."

Mr. Black lowered his arm and handed his gun to Jehu. He looked up into the sky, squinting. And then he said, "I best be going, Obediah."

Mr. Russell nodded slightly. "Watch yer topknot," he said.

"Watch yourn." Mr. Black tipped his hat and walked away.

CHAPTER EIGHTEEN
or,
A Patch of Land

Kur-ukso's new friend, Spaark, let us travel in her family's canoe, so the journey home was completed in two easy days.

"You're gonna be the death of me, Jane," Jehu said in a low voice, as we paddled along. He was furious with me. "What if Black had shot you?"

"But he didn't," I said, and I was grateful.

Jehu and the other men had come looking for me when Mr. Russell and I had not turned up. And while I was thankful that they had saved Mr. Russell's life, I was thankful for other things, too.

However, we had returned to the negotiations just in time to see them fall apart one final time.

The governor, who had clearly woken up irritable, immediately launched into Tleyuk, yelling at him quite forcefully and blaming him for starting all the fights the evening before. And then before the startled Tleyuk could say anything in his own defense, the governor, in front of everybody, ripped up the piece of paper the government had given Tleyuk recognizing him as *tyee*.

The whole of the campground went silent in astonishment that the governor would insult a *tyee* in such a manner. I glanced over and saw that William had a most disconcertingly satisfied look on his face.

But Tleyuk was deadly calm. In a quiet voice, he told the governor that he still spoke for his people and that there would be no treaty. And before the governor could react, Indians from most of the assembled tribes were starting to leave: the meeting was over.

William's stunned expression at this pronouncement was priceless. His machinations had come to naught. Now there would be no reservation for anyone in the near future.

So it was a very happy and boisterous party that left for our little settlement on Shoalwater Bay. Mr. Russell's cabin seemed like a warm, glowing beacon in the middle of a storm. Father Joseph, M'Carty, and Cocumb were waiting for us when we returned—tired and cranky, and rather smelly, I confess.

"Jehu! Keer-ukso!" Cocumb said, relief clear on her face. "We were so worried."

"She's just buttering us up to finish that roof, eh?" Jehu teased, nudging Keer-ukso in the ribs.

I was enveloped in a hug of warm wool.

"Mademoiselle," Father Joseph said, his voice catching.

I blinked in surprise at the emotion rushing through me at this show of affection.

"Good to have ya back, Russell!" M'Carty roared, clapping Mr. Russell on the back.

Mr. Russell grinned at him like a young boy. "Good to be back!"

Brandywine leaped up, licking me, and then little Sootie was gripping my leg. I just stood there and smiled into Jehu's blue eyes.

That first night back is one I shall never forget.

"A party!" Mr. Swan proposed.

Mr. Russell's cabin had never seemed as warm and welcoming in all the months I had been there, nor the company so perfect. I remember the sweet sound of laughter, and Brandywine's happy barks, and how Mr. Swan pulled out a fiddle and struck up a tune and Jehu swung me around and around, and my heart filled to bursting with happiness. In that moment as I was being spun in the arms of the man who loved my ratty, tangled hair, I knew I had found a family as loving and warm and dear as Papa and Mrs. Parker. A rather eccentric family, I conceded, but still, I rather think Papa would have approved of such a group, outlaws every one.

And then Mr. Russell, to everyone's surprise, pulled me out to dance, and swung me around skillfully. The glowing fire shined on his face, turning his gray beard red, and for a brief moment I saw what he must have looked like as a young man, all earnest and eager to find his fortune in the mountains of the unknown frontier.

"You're a fine dancer," I complimented as he dipped and twirled and spun me until I was dizzy.

"And yar a fine gal," he said softly, his eyes serious.

It was the closest to thanks I would ever get for saving his life, but those few words meant more to me than the sweetest flattery from the most accomplished gentleman's lips.

And perhaps, I thought, that was what being a lady was all about—knowing the true value of a gift.

The next morning found me in the cabin sewing clothes for the rag doll I had never given to Sootie. If I gave it some proper clothes, it would look good enough to give to her, although it would never be as fine as the china doll from Mrs. Frink.

There was a soft knock on the cabin door.

"Come in," I called, never looking up.

"Oh, Miss Peck, you're back! We were all so concerned about you," Mrs. Frink said. She stood hesitantly in the doorway, the light framing her petite figure.

I managed a small smile. "Please come in."

"I milked Burton while you were away," she said. "The poor dear was mooing so loudly that Mr. Frink and I could barely sleep."

I winced.

She was smiling at me in her earnest way. "What is that you're working on?"

"A doll," I said reluctantly. "For Sootie."

"How very clever of you!"

Mrs. Frink came over, studying my handiwork. She eyed the small wardrobe I had sewn thus far: a calico dress, an apron, a cloak, a nightdress. She clapped her hands together happily. "I know just the thing." She disappeared from the cabin, returning a moment later with a small bundle in her hands.

"Here," she said, thrusting it forward.

I took it reluctantly. I untied the bundle, and out spilled velvet and soft linen and smooth silks. There were ornate, tiny, beautifully embroidered dresses. There were perfect knitted caps. Socks and mittens and crisp nightdresses. Everything a fashionable, well-dressed doll could desire.

"I adore this one," Mrs. Frink said, fingering a peach velvet smock with cross-stitch embroidery around the hem. "It took ages to sew the lace on just right."

She must have labored for months and months to create these perfect little clothes. The calico dress I had sewn looked crude next to them. The cloak pathetic. The apron like the handkerchief it was. Had I truly expected to best Mrs. Frink? A sense of despair welled up in me as I looked from each perfect piece to the next.

Mrs. Frink had not stopped talking. "I dearly hope our furniture arrives soon," she said.

"Furniture?"

"Why, yes. I had our furniture shipped around the cape. Mr. Frink was quite insistent that we travel overland to get here. He so wanted to see the country, but I tell you, I very much wish we had gone by sea. I prefer a sea voyage any day. I'm a good sailor," she finished firmly.

"I came on a ship," I said, not wanting to add that I had spent most of the voyage puking into a bucket.

Mrs. Frink studied me, stroking a small pair of socks. "You're from Philadelphia, aren't you? I thought I recognized the accent. Do you have relations there still?"

My throat felt thick. "My papa's dead. He was all I ever had."

Mrs. Frink's hand slowly put the socks back in the pile. "I am very sorry for your loss, Miss Peck."

I couldn't stop the bitter words that escaped my lips.

"I'm all alone," I said.

A shadow passed over Mrs. Frink's flushed face. "Oh, my dear, we are never alone. Even when we lose a loved one, we must remember that they are still there watching us. Why, I tell Mr. Frink that all the time. 'Mr. Frink,' I say, 'I believe our little baby Lila is smiling down at us from heaven even though she is buried beneath that rock on the trail west of Fort Laramie. Yes, she is in heaven, and she is smiling down on us this very moment, so there is no reason to cry.'"

Her smile was strained, and it didn't reach her eyes.

"Oh," I said. I looked down at the tiny clothes in my hand. These weren't doll clothes at all. They were baby clothes. For a baby who would never wear them.

I looked up at Mrs. Frink, a woman I had thought perfect, and something in me softened. I had been wrong about her, too.

"I'm so sorry, Mrs. Frink. Truly I am." I wanted to say I was sorry for misjudging her, but I think she knew.

"So am I, Miss Peck," she whispered, her lower lip trembling. "More than I can ever say."

"I believe these shall make Sootie very happy," I said, smoothing one of the tiny embroidered dresses.

"I'm so very glad," she said, swallowing hard. "And you must please call me Matilda."

"I shall, Matilda," I said. "If you will call me Jane."

Mrs. Frink nodded, marshaling her charm.

"Well then, Jane, I was wondering if you would be willing to help me with something." She clasped her hands together and leaned forward confidingly. "I'm afraid that I'm quite desperate for the good opinion of another lady."

Mrs. Frink hired me to help run the hotel.

I would be specifically in charge of designing the menu of the dining room, and acting as local liaison. The hotel's initial clientele would be new settlers and gentlemen looking for opportunities in the territory, but the Frinks were quite optimistic that the hotel would attract tourists in time.

"After all," Mrs. Frink declared, "who can resist the beautiful beach?"

The hotel was scheduled to open its doors to guests in the early spring. In the meantime, I would be kept busy assisting Mrs. Frink in outfitting the guest rooms with linen and wallpaper and all manner of things that we ordered from California.

She wanted my opinions on all these matters, and I found that my education at Miss Hepplewhite's Young Ladies Academy, which had been generally of little use on the frontier, proved indispensable in this regard.

One afternoon as I started out for the hotel to look at a new set of fabric swatches that had arrived, Jehu grabbed my arm.

"You're coming with me!" he announced.

"I have to go to see Mrs. Frink," I protested.

"I informed her that you had a very important engagement," he said mysteriously.

He dragged me out to his plot of land by the bay. It was a cool January day, and the wind was whipping us along.

"This is it," Jehu said as we stood on the cliff he had brought me to mere months ago.

"Yes, I know. What did you bring me out here for?"

"I have my reasons," he said, and slapped a folded piece of paper in my hand.

"What's this?"

"Read it, Jane," he urged, a note of excitement in his voice.

I carefully unfolded the paper.

GRANT FOR ONE HUNDRED AND TWENTY
ACRES OF LAND TO J. PECK. DECEMBER 22, 1854.

When I looked up, his eyes were dancing. "Well? How do you like your patch of land?"

"My land?"

"Yes, your land. That's a land grant for you. Thought I'd build you a house of your own. Mine'll be over here," he said, pointing. "And then in time, maybe we could"—here he cleared his throat nervously—"well, you know."

I looked at Jehu, astonished by the depth of the misunderstanding. That day when he had brought me up here, he had not been trying to marry me for land. He had been trying to help me claim a piece of land for my own—next to his claim, so I wouldn't feel scared or nervous, but my land all the same.

I studied the document more closely. "J. Peck?"

"They'll never know. You could be a Jonathan or a Jack or a Jebediah—"

"Or a Jane," I finished dryly.

He leaned over and kissed me so softly that for a moment all I heard was the roaring of the waves . . . or was it my heart? "You'll never be just a Jane to me."

"I've never been a landowner before," I said.

"I'm sure you'll rise to the occasion," he teased gently.

I smiled and looked at my patch of land.

My land.

The fog was rolling in from the bay, but in spite of the chill in the air I felt warm clear through. This wild, rough, tumbling wilderness that had once seemed so terribly cold and unfriendly now burgeoned with hope and enterprise and friendship. And I can't be sure, but I swear I heard a voice in the waves crashing on the rocks below.

Home, it whispered.

"I believe I would like the porch right here," I announced, my feet curling on the edge of the cliff. Jehu caught me to him, tucking his chin on my head, his arm safely anchoring my waist.

"Fine place for a porch," he murmured.

I elbowed him gently. "And perhaps a garden over there?"

He stifled a grin. "I know just the man to dig it out."

I stared out at the bay rolling in, the gulls kissing the waves.

"I've been wondering about something," I said.

"Hmmm?"

I turned to him, tracing the scar on his cheek gently. "What did you mean when you said that Mr. Russell was right about me?"

Jehu chuckled, smoothing my hand flat to his cheek. He pressed a kiss in the palm.

"Stop trying to distract me," I said, giving him a little push. "Tell me."

Jehu Scudder, the blue-eyed sailor who had stolen my heart, shook his head and smiled. "He said, 'That gal is full of spit.'"

"Spit?"

He winked, and then said in a fair imitation of Mr. Russell, "And yar, gal."

The Frink Hotel opened its doors to great fanfare in late winter.

There was an opening day gala, and I was complimented by everyone on the beautifully appointed rooms as well as the delicious food. Mrs. Frink announced that my pies were to be the signature dessert of the hotel.

Winter seemed to pass in a heartbeat, and spring arrived on the bay, bringing with it rainy days and settlers. New people seemed to be arriving daily, and not just men anymore. There were now several families, with women and children, as well as a real doctor. Small houses were springing up everywhere. We were full to capacity at the hotel, and Father Joseph was thrilled to have so many new parishioners to attend his church.

Jehu, who now acted as the harbor's pilot, guiding the arriving vessels through the many shoals, was building my house bit by bit. We spent our evenings in the cozy parlor of the hotel, where I was living until my house was ready. Jehu and Keer-ukso intended to start a sawmill business together but needed capital to do so. Jehu was planning to go to San Francisco sometime soon to find an investor for their venture.

Spaark was a frequent guest at Chief Toke's lodge, and on occasion she helped me at the hotel, where I enjoyed her company very much. She didn't speak English yet, but I spoke the Jargon well enough to carry on conversation. She confided in me that while she found Keer-ukso very easy on the eye, it was his sense of humor that attracted her.

"Sense of humor?" I asked.

She nodded seriously, her eyes dancing. "He is most funny. He tells stories about you, Boston Jane," she confessed with a giggle.

"Stories?" I asked, alarmed.

"Skunk stories," she said, and then burst into peals of laughter.

At Mrs. Frink's urging, I gave Sootie the rag doll I'd made.

The little girl was thrilled, and now often gave tea parties for both her dolls. Sootie adored the china doll, but it was the rag doll she dragged by the arm everywhere she went—so much so that the poor doll often lost its appendages and I was prevailed upon to doctor it.

I confess, the sight of that armless doll warmed my heart as nothing else ever could.

"Jane," Mrs. Frink said, looking up from the ledger she was writing in. "Would you mind going down to the beach? There's a schooner arriving that should have those extra dishes we ordered. If they're broken, I want them sent back directly on the same ship. Jehu's down there already."

I was in the kitchen experimenting on a new concoction. Salmonberry jam.

"Of course," I said, wiping my hands on my apron, happy for the opportunity to be outside on a day like this. As I made my way down to the beach, I passed Mr. Swan.

"Hello, my dear," he said. "Capital day, don't you think?"

"It's simply beautiful," I agreed.

Mr. Swan cleared his throat nervously. "Actually, I was looking for you."

"Yes?"

He handed me a piece of paper.

"What is this?" I asked.

"The deed to the oyster bed. My dear, I am ashamed to say that I shall never be able to repay you for the money that I, well"—here he swallowed hard—"gambled away."

I looked at Mr. Swan and remembered how his voice had shaken with fear when he'd defended me from Mr. Black.

"Mr. Swan," I sighed, handing him back the deed. "I shall never find a partner as good as you."

"But my dear, I ruined everything—"

"No," I said firmly, patting his hand. "We are partners. I'm sure you can find some other way to pay back the money."

"Are you sure, my dear?" he asked, a hopeful smile wreathing his face.

"A lady always knows her own mind, Mr. Swan."

He breathed a sigh of relief.

"Although I believe that *I* shall hold the money from now on," I added as an afterthought.

He had the good grace to look sheepish.

And then we both laughed.

"Where are you off to?" he asked finally.

"The beach. There's a schooner arriving with some dishes we ordered from San Francisco."

"Oh yes," he said, his white beard shining in the sun. "And there are some passengers on the schooner, too, I believe."

I smiled. "We'll be a regular town in no time."

"Yes, yes. I imagine we shall even have to have some elections soon."

"Elections?"

"For mayor, judge, et cetera," he said, rubbing his beard thoughtfully.

"You'd make a wonderful mayor," I said.

His eyes lit up at this suggestion. "Do you really think so?"

"Yes, I really do," I said. "Now I must go. The boat will be arriving."

As I walked away, I heard him murmur to himself in a bemused voice, "Mayor? What a capital idea."

A light wind was whipping across the beach, bringing with it the scent of the sea. In the distance a schooner had weighed anchor, and cargo and passengers were being lowered into Jehu's waiting rowboat.

Sootie was perched on a boulder, playing with a small grouping of dolls. In addition to my doll and Mrs. Frink's doll, there were two new dolls—one fashioned from a clamshell and a rag doll most certainly acquired from one of the pioneer children.

"You sure have a lot of dolls there," I said, taking in the small pile.

"Yes," she said in a satisfied little voice. "I traded. I have more dolls than any other girl. I am very rich."

"I see," I said.

Sootie grinned up at me. "But I like yours best."

Chief Toke came walking over to us, and I nodded in greeting. He ruffled his daughter's silky hair.

Sootie had piled a bunch of small pebbles in front of one of the dolls and was elaborately giving pebbles to the other dolls.

"What are you playing?" I asked, curious.

"*Potlatch.*"

"What's that?"

Chief Toke cleared his throat and said, "*Potlatch* is ceremony giving gifts. Give everything away to guests."

"But why would you give everything away?" I asked confused. "Then you will have nothing."

"You give things away, and new things will be given to you," he said simply.

"Boston Jane," Sootie said urgently, "will you make new dress for this doll?" She waved the new rag doll. "With buttons, too."

I met Chief Toke's eyes over Sootie's head and smiled. Perhaps he was right. I might have lost everything, but I had found more than I ever expected.

"You come to lodge for supper," Chief Toke said firmly.

"Of course," I said.

"Come, Sootie," he said, lifting her to the ground and helping her gather her dolls.

"I'll help you with the dress tomorrow," I promised Sootie.

As they walked away, Chief Toke paused and turned to me. "Boston Jane, will you make me shirt like Jehu?"

"The blue calico one?"

"It is good shirt." And here he winked. "Jehu won't trade it."

I smiled at him and watched as father and daughter climbed over the dunes, heading home. I perched on Sootie's boulder to wait, looking out at the bay, at the fast-moving clouds dancing across the sky. It seemed so strange to think that I was now a resident and landowner of this gentle stretch of wilderness.

A rowboat was winging its way to shore through the waves; at its head I spotted Jehu's familiar black hair. The settlers in the boat waved and shouted to me. I went down to the edge of the water to greet them, recalling how months before I had stood on this very same stretch of beach with my trunk packed, prepared to return to Philadelphia.

When I was a child on Walnut Street, happiness had been the sound of Papa's voice.

But here, a continent away, at the edge of the wilderness, happiness was Jehu's gruff laugh, and Sootie's excited shout, and even the sound of Mr. Russell spitting.

I was the luckiest girl in the world.

I heard everything now—the hum of the land, the soothing waves, and the excitement in the voices of the settlers with their hope for a new life. Yet one sound rang clear through above all others.

A voice screeched across the water, sharp as glass.

"Jane Peck!"

I swear, my heart stopped beating.

Standing in the middle of the rowboat, blond curls flying in the wind, head straining forward, was someone I truly thought I'd never see again in all my born days.

Miss Sally Biddle of Philadelphia.

The End

AUTHOR'S NOTE

I really got into the spirit of this book. In addition to the usual research, I actually made what James Swan describes as "a fisherman's pudding," and found it quite tasty (if a little sweet!).

Here are some other ways real life and research influenced Jane's story:

The Stevens negotiations actually did take place, but later, in February of 1855. The Cowlitz, Chinook, Chehalis, and Shoalwater Bay tribes did not sign the Stevens treaty. James Swan attended the negotiations and described them in his book, *The Northwest Coast, Or Three Years' Residence in Washington Territory*. Shoalwater Bay is known as Willapa Bay today.

The character of Mrs. Frink was inspired by, but not based on, an actual pioneer woman, Margaret Frink, who traveled from Indiana to California in 1850 for the Gold Rush. You can read an actual account of Mr. and Mrs. Frink's difficult journey in her diary, published as *Covered Wagon Women, Diaries & Letters from the Western Trails, 1850*.

The fur trade, whose heyday ran from the early 1800s until

the early 1840s, was driven by fashion. Gentlemen's hats made of beaver fur were all the rage, but like all fashion fads, the hats eventually lost favor. However, the myth of the fur trapper, or mountain man, grew to heroic proportions. To learn more about the hardships and high adventures of mountain men, contact the Museum of the Fur Trade, 6321 Highway 20, Chadron, NE 69337.

RESOURCES

Chehalis Tribal Office, Oakville, Washington.

Chinook Tribal Office, Chinook, Washington.

Museum of the Fur Trade, Chadron, Nebraska.

Pacific County Historical Society and Museum, South Bend, Washington.

Covered Wagon Women: Diaries & Letters from the Western Trails, 1850, edited and compiled by Kenneth L. Holmes, University of Nebraska Press.

The Northwest Coast, Or Three Years' Residence in Washington Territory, James G. Swan, University of Washington Press.

A Rendezvous Reader: Tall, Tangled, and True Tales of the Mountain Men 1805–1850, edited by James H. Maguire, Peter Wild, and Donald A. Barclay, University of Utah Press.

ABOUT THE AUTHOR

Jennifer L. Holm is the author of two Newbery Honor books, *Our Only May Amelia* and *Penny from Heaven*. She is also the author of several other highly praised books, including the Boston Jane trilogy, *Middle School Is Worse Than Meatloaf,* and the Babymouse series, which she collaborates on with her brother Matthew Holm. Jennifer lives in California with her husband and two children. You can visit her Web site at www.jenniferholm.com.

Don't miss book three
in the Boston Jane trilogy

Coming from Yearling in September 2010!
Turn the page for a preview.

CHAPTER ONE
or,
Old Ghosts

I was standing on a high bluff looking out at the vast shimmering sweep of blue-green water that was Shoal-water Bay.

Spring was in bloom, with drizzly rains and soft nights, and occasionally, a glorious day such as this one—when the sun broke out from behind the clouds and brushed the lush green wilderness with a golden tint. A sweet, salty wind swept over the waves, sending my thick, curly red hair flying in all directions. Gulls swooped and cried like nosy neighbors, diving low to the water. I should have been strolling through town, enjoying this rare and dazzling May day. Unfortunately, I was not feeling very well.

As a matter of fact, I was puking.

I had thought she was a ghost, perched behind Jehu in the back of a rowboat heading toward shore. I wished she were a ghost.

I retched again, but there was nothing left in my stomach.

Sally Biddle. With her wealthy family and faultless manners, she had been the belle of Philadelphia society when I lived there. But beneath her blond ringlets and fashionable gowns, she was a perfect monster, one whose chief amusement was tormenting other girls. Or at least one girl. Me. She had contrived to make my childhood a misery. And whenever I had earned small victories, Sally had always made me pay for them tenfold.

Trust me, you would puke, too.

Sally was one of the reasons I had been so eager to leave Philadelphia to put an entire continent between us. And now, here she was. What possible reason could my childhood tormentor have for following me to the farthest reaches of the Washington Territory? It made no sense. Had she traveled all this way just to torture me?

But there was no denying it. She was real. No ghost would wear such an elegant dress with a matching cape and smart bonnet. Why, Sally looked as if she were on her way to tea, and not arriving from a sea voyage of several months. She looked perfect, as usual, not at all like the seasick mess I had been upon my arrival more than a year earlier.

When Jehu's rowboat had hit the sandy beach, the sick feeling in the pit of my stomach exploded, and a single thought thrummed in my head: *Sally Biddle is here!*

Sally had stood up and held out a hand to Jehu, and the sight of that gloved hand resting on Jehu's strong arm as he helped her to shore had shaken me like nothing else could. I had done the only thing a lady could do in such a situation. I had picked up my skirts and run all the way up here to the high bluff to be sick in private.

Now, with each breath of crisp air, I felt my stomach settle and a measure of calm return to me. I was on my claim, I told myself over and over, like a litany. Behind me was the beginning of the beautiful new home my sweet Jehu was building me. Nothing bad could happen to me here.

Something in the distance caught my eye. A blond-haired figure was slowly strolling through the woods, pausing here and there. At first glance I feared Sally Biddle had followed me, but then I saw that it was clearly a man, and not a lady.

"Boston Jane!" a voice cried from the other direction.

I turned to see little Sootie and her cousin Katy barreling toward me, dolls in tow. When I looked back to where the figure had been, he was gone, vanished into the thick dark woods.

"We've been looking everywhere for you!" Sootie exclaimed in a rush.

Sootie was a whirligig of energy. With her thick black hair, copper skin, and bright, excited eyes, the daughter of Chief Toke of the Chinook tribe took after her mother, my friend Suis, who had died in the smallpox epidemic the previous year.

"Star's has new fabric! It just arrived on the schooner!" she exclaimed in a rush, waving her rag doll at me.

Sootie, like her mother before her, was a skilled trader, and she had amassed a small collection of dolls from other children of the settlement through her skillful dealings. I had promised her that I would make a dress for this latest doll.

"Why are you all the way out here?" Katy asked curiously.

Katy, the eleven-year-old daughter of a local pioneer and his Chinook wife, had inherited the fair skin of her father and the brown eyes and lustrous black hair of her mother. She was an uncommonly beautiful little girl with a gentle disposition that I found charming.

"I'm hiding from a *memelose*," I said lightly.

"A *memelose*?" Katy asked in hushed tones, looking around nervously. "Really?"

Memelose was the Chinook word for spirit.

"You should change your name, Boston Jane," Sootie said, all seriousness. "Then the *memelose* won't be able to find you."

The Chinook believed that if you changed your name, you could outwit a *memelose* who wanted to lure you to the other side. And in a manner of speaking, I had done just that. I was now known to many here on the bay as Boston Jane, a name bestowed upon me by my Chinook friends and dear to me for what it implied. Boston Jane was a woman of courage. She had survived and endured in the wilderness, carving a place for herself in this fragile settlement at the edge of the frontier. But I knew that I could change my name a thousand times and it would not alter the fact that Sally Biddle was here on Shoalwater Bay.

"The *memelose* has already found me," I said.

Sootie considered this for a moment, then declared bravely, "I'm not afraid of *memeloses*!"

I wanted to tell her that Sally Biddle was one *memelose* she should fear.

"Don't worry, Boston Jane," Katy said. "We'll protect you!"

"She's not really a *memelose*," I admitted. "She's just a girl." A rather disagreeable girl, I wanted to add.

"You can tell us the truth, Boston Jane. We're not afraid," Katy said.

"I wish she weren't real," I murmured.

They nodded.

"Now come to town," Sootie said, tugging at my arm. "Before all the fabric is gone!"

I looked out at the sparkling bay and sighed. I couldn't very well hide forever, could I? I brushed off my hands on my skirt, tugged my bonnet over my wild red curls, and stood up.

"Very well," I agreed, and then gave them a small wink. "But if Sally Biddle comes to haunt me, I'm sending her after you!"

Mr. Russell's raggedy little cabin marked the far edge of our burgeoning settlement.

Pioneers came to Shoalwater Bay lured by stories of oyster farming, and land for homesteading. Our town was growing right along the shore, making it most convenient for the hardworking oystermen who toiled on the bay. Many of the homes were built on pilings and floats to survive the sometimes perilously high tides. In some places the cabins were scarcely more than shacks, and tents were visible as well. While there were several families in residence now, most of our inhabitants were unmarried men, which was why, I supposed, we had three taverns and a coffin shop but no schools.

Mr. Russell's cabin, though, was sensibly placed far above

the high-water mark, in a clearing in the woods. When I'd first arrived, this ramshackle cabin was the only true house the settlement had to offer. It was my first home here. Unfortunately, it had also been home to every filthy, flea-bitten prospecting man who happened to be passing through. Mr. Russell was not generally given to cleanliness, and his cabin usually reflected this personal trait. At the moment, the bewhiskered, buckskin-clad mountain man was sitting on the porch.

"Hello, Mr. Russell," I called, and waved.

He spit a wad of tobacco in my general direction and waved back to us.

Mr. Russell and I had been through a lot together, and I felt a tremendous fondness for the man. I'll admit I even felt a bit homesick for that wretched dirt-floor shack of his.

The girls and I passed the cabin and set off along the main road that led down to the center of town. I was immediately barraged by the familiar scents and sounds that characterized Front Street—raucous shouts emanating from one of the taverns, the tangy smell of manure mixed with mud, the sharp salty breeze off the bay, oystermen dickering over prices, the murmurs of men discussing whether or not it would rain.

Front Street, which ran parallel to shore, was a rather grand title for a path that was usually little more than a swath of thick, boot-sticking mud. A ramshackle, narrow walkway, constructed of spare planks salvaged from shipwrecks and packing crates, ran alongside this muddy route. My young companions ran nimbly along the walkway, dancing ahead of me.

"Hurry, Boston Jane," Sootie shouted over her shoulder. "All the fabric will be gone!"

Front Street was crowded with all manner of men. There were Indians from local tribes, pioneers from back east, miners who had not struck gold in California and wanted to try their chances on oysters, and men who were fleeing the law. In short, our citizens consisted mainly of rough-and-tumble men who could not be bothered to build proper houses or bathe but happily drank their earnings. It was altogether a wild community, especially after dark.

Wagons full of freshly harvested oysters hauled their cargo up and down the muddy thoroughfare. Here and there, men were holding friendly wagers by tossing gold coins in the sand. Oysters were making men rich. The native bivalves were in such demand in San Francisco that men thought nothing of paying a silver dollar for a fresh-shucked oyster.

Even I was part of the oyster rush. I owned a canoe and oyster beds with my friend Mr. Swan, although our business had not been too successful of late. My partner had gambled away the profits from the last harvest. As I was increasingly busy with my duties at the hotel where I worked, I was considering renting out the beds to another oysterman for a share of the profits.

Ahead of me a man stood lounging on the narrow walkway, making it impossible for me to pass.

"Excuse me," I said.

But the man, who had clearly been spending his oyster money on whiskey, simply leered at me.

I was forced to step onto the road, where I soon found myself ankle-deep in mud. After several boot-clogging steps, I passed the man and climbed back onto the walkway.

Farther down the muddy thoroughfare, I spied the gay bunting of Star's Dry Goods, and beyond that the outline of the Frink Hotel.

Sootie bounded up the steps of Star's in front of me, while Katy hovered behind.

"Boston Jane, what if the *memelose* girl is here?" Katy asked in a whisper. "*Memeloses* are very dangerous! They can hurt you because no one can see them."

"We'll be fine," I assured her with more courage than I felt.

She eyed me warily.

A small brass bell attached to the door rang as we entered.

Star's Dry Goods was a jumble of goods stacked floor to ceiling. There were harness fittings, bird seed, molasses, nails, flour, tea, coffee, and even umbrellas—the most practical item in the store, considering the amount of rain Shoalwater Bay received. The huge barrel of molasses sat alongside a barrel of hard cider and one of vinegar. Glass jars filled with candy waited hopefully for small children to sample their wares. In addition to the standard store items, Mr. Staroselsky's wife ordered goods that were appreciated by the ladies. There was a very nice assortment of fabrics, as well as sewing needles, ribbon, buttons, hosiery, cotton yarns, and combs. It was all arranged in a haphazard fashion that only Mr. Staroselsky seemed to know how to navigate.

In the back of the room, several men sat in captain's chairs around the small potbellied stove. It was a favorite place to exchange gossip.

"Hello, Jane," Mrs. Staroselsky called from behind the counter.

Mrs. Staroselsky, a vibrant young woman with a tumble of thick, black curly hair, could often be seen making deliveries around town for her husband. She had a brand-new baby named Rose, who was presently in her arms and making quite a fuss.

Sootie pushed in front of me to the counter. "Boston Jane is going to buy us some of the new fabric for our dolls!"

"For new dresses!" Katy added.

"Well, aren't you girls lucky," Mrs. Staroselsky said, smiling at me over Sootie's head. "I saw Jehu with an enormous wagon of luggage. New arrivals?"

Jehu acted as the pilot for the bay, guiding ships in through the shoals and helping them unload their goods.

"Yes," I said. "From Philadelphia."

"How wonderful for you to have folks here from back home," Mrs. Staroselsky said.

I bit my lip.

"Can I hold the baby?" Sootie asked, scrambling up to peer at the whimpering baby in Mrs. Staroselsky's arms.

"You may," Mrs. Staroselsky said, passing her the restless bundle. "Perhaps you can calm her down. She's been crying for days."

I nodded sympathetically.

"Look, she's not crying anymore!" Sootie said in a hushed voice as she carefully rocked the baby. "She likes me!"

And indeed, Rose was staring up at Sootie's face with something approaching wonder.

Mrs. Staroselsky and I smiled over the girls' heads.

"Maybe you should keep Rose for a while, Sootie," Mrs. Staroselsky said with a wink.

I left Sootie and Katy at Star's, minding the baby, and continued down Front Street toward the Frink Hotel, passing one of the local taverns, which doubled as a bowling alley.

The tavern was situated inside an abandoned Chinook lodge, and shouting and revelry could be heard there until all hours of the night. Men seemed to lose all good sense when whiskey was involved, and there was a great deal of whiskey available on Shoalwater Bay, thanks to Red Charley. Red Charley had grown rich in his whiskey dealings and liked to go about town with a woolen sock full of gold coins tied to his belt. The whiskey-dealing devil himself was lolling outside the bowling alley on an empty barrel as I walked by.

"Lookee there," Red Charley chortled. "It's Jane Peck! When're you gonna get rid of that sailor fella, huh?"

Red Charley was referring to Jehu, who was a seasoned sailor and captain. He had been first mate on the *Lady Luck*, the ship that had brought me to Shoalwater Bay.

Red Charley turned to the filthy prospecting fellow lazing next to him and said, "I keep telling her I'll marry her! What does Jehu got that I don't?" He followed his question with a belch. "I sure am a lot more handsome."

I raised an eyebrow at this. With his huge belly, red cheeks, and terrible disposition, Red Charley was hardly a young lady's dream.

"How's he going to support you puttering around in that wee boat?" another man shouted.

"How do ya know he hasn't got a wife in some other port? Now, an oysterman like me'll stay put," a man with a missing tooth assured me with a lopsided smile.

"He ain't worth love," Red Chancy cackled. "The only thing worth that kind of hankering is Old Rye!"

"Good day," I said firmly, and continued on, dragging my now muddy skirts behind me.

Farther down the street I arrived at the Frink Hotel. Outside it stood a horse-drawn wagon piled high with trunks, and helping to unload the wagon was the dark-haired sailor Red Charley had been talking about.

"Jehu!" I called happily.

He turned to me, his eyes lighting up, his smile tugging at my heart. He was so handsome, with his shock of curly black hair, his blue eyes, the scar that ran jaggedly along his cheek.

"Jane," he said.

At that moment the door to the hotel opened and Sally Biddle appeared, wearing a rose silk dress and a smug expression.

"Why, if it isn't Jane Peck! What a marvelous coincidence!" Sally trilled, her gold curls shining in the sun.

Jehu grinned at me, setting down the trunk he was carrying. "It'll be good to have an old friend out here, won't it, Jane?"

I had never spoken to Jehu of Sally Biddle. In truth, I had hoped to forget her completely.

"Yes, Jane. I was just telling Mr. Scudder what great friends we were in Philadelphia," Sally said sweetly, the very model of a kind girlfriend, her gaze lingering just a moment too long on Jehu's handsome features. "We had such wonderful times together, didn't we?"

I saw the look in Sally's eyes daring me to contradict her, and my stomach roiled. Katy was right to have warned me. Sally Biddle was just as dangerous as any *memelose*—and no one but me could see her true self. I felt my face go cold, my skin prickle with sweat.

"Jane," Sally said, her eyes mock-solicitous. "Are you feeling well? You look rather . . . drawn."

"Jane?" Jehu asked, concern in his voice.

But I couldn't answer. I turned and fled up the stairs of the hotel to my room.